The Rider on the White Horse

The Rider on the White Horse

by Theodor Storm

©2008 Wilder Publications

Wilder Publications, LLC.
PO Box 3005
Radford VA 24143-3005

ISBN 10: 1515433005
ISBN 13: 9781515433002

What I am about to tell I learned nearly half a century ago in the house of my great-grand-mother, old Madame Fedderson, widow of the senator, while I was sitting beside her armchair, busy reading a magazine bound in blue pasteboard—I don't remember whether it was a copy of the "Leipzig" or of "Pappes Hamburger Lesefrüchte." I still remember with a shudder how meanwhile the light hand of the past eighty-year-old woman glided tenderly over the hair of her great-grandson. She herself and her time are buried long ago. In vain have I searched for that magazine, and therefore I am even less able to vouch for the truth of the statements in it than I am to defend them if anyone should question them; but of so much I can assure anyone, that since that time they have never been forgotten, even though no outer incident has revived them in my memory.

It was in the third decade of our century, on an October afternoon—thus began the story-teller of that time—that I rode through a mighty storm along a North Frisian dike. For over an hour I had on my left the dreary marshland, already deserted by all the cattle; on my right, unpleasantly near me, the swamping waters of the North Sea. I saw nothing, however, but the yellowish-grey waves that beat against the dike unceasingly, as if they were roaring with rage, and that now and then bespattered me and my horse with dirty foam; behind them I could see only chaotic dusk which did not let me tell sky and earth apart, for even the half moon which now stood in the sky was most of the time covered by wandering clouds. It was ice cold; my clammy hands could scarcely hold the reins, and I did not wonder that the croaking and cackling crows and gulls were always letting themselves be swept inland by the storm. Nightfall had begun, and already I could no longer discern the hoof of my horse with any certainty. I had met no human soul, heard nothing but the screaming of the birds when they almost grazed me and my faithful mare with their long wings, and the raging of the wind and water. I cannot deny that now and then I wished that I were in safe quarters.

It was the third day that this weather had lasted, and I had already allowed an especially dear relative to keep me longer than I should have done on his estate in one of the more northern districts. But to-day I could not stay longer. I had business in the city which was even now a few hours' ride to the south, and in spite of all the persuasions of my cousin and his kind wife, in spite of the Perinette and Grand Richard apples still to be tried, I had ridden away.

"Wait till you get to the sea," he had called after me from his house door. "You will turn back. Your room shall be kept for you."

And really, for a moment, when a black layer of clouds spread pitch-darkness round me and at the same time the howling squalls were trying to force me and my horse down from the dike, the thought shot through my head: "Don't be a fool! Turn back and stay with your friends in their warm nest." But then it occurred to me that the way back would be longer than the way to my destination; and so I trotted on, pulling the collar of my coat up over my ears.

But now something came toward me upon the dike; I heard nothing, but when the half moon shed its spare light, I believed that I could discern more and more clearly a dark figure, and soon, as it drew nearer, I saw that it sat on a horse, on a long-legged, haggard, white horse; a dark cloak was waving round its shoulders, and as it flew past me, two glowing eyes stared at me out of a pale face.

Who was that? What did that man want? And now it came to my mind that I had not heard the beating of hoofs or any panting of the horse; and yet horse and rider had ridden close by me!

Deep in thought over this I rode on, but I did not have much time to think, for straightway it flew past me again from behind; it seemed as if the flying cloak had grazed me, as if the apparition, just as it had done the first time, had rushed by me without a sound. Then I saw it farther and farther away from me, and suddenly it seemed as if a shadow were gliding down at the inland side of the dike.

Somewhat hesitating, I rode on behind. When I had reached that place, hard by the "Koog," the land won from the sea by damming it in, I saw water gleam from a great "Wehl," as they call the breaks made into the land by the storm floods which remain as small but deep pools.

In spite of the protecting dike, the water was remarkably calm; hence the rider could not have troubled it. Besides, I saw nothing more of him. Something else I saw now, however, which I greeted with pleasure: before me, from out of the "Koog," a multitude of little scattered lights were glimmering up to me; they seemed to come from some of the rambling Frisian houses that lay isolated on more or less high mounds. But close in front of me, half way up the inland side of the dike lay a great house of this kind. On the south side, to the right of the house door, I saw all the windows illumined, and beyond, I perceived people and imagined that I could hear them in spite of the storm. My horse had of himself walked down to the road along the dike which led me up to the door of the house. I could easily see that it was a tavern, for in front of the windows I spied the so-called "ricks," beams resting on two posts with great iron rings for hitching the cattle and horses that stopped there.

I tied my horse to one of these and left him to the servant who met me as I entered the hall.

"Is a meeting going on here?" I asked him, for now a noise of voices and clicking glasses rose clearly from the room beyond the door.

"Aye, something of the sort," the servant replied in Plattdeutsch, and later I learned that this dialect had been in full swing here, as well as the Frisian, for over a hundred years; "the dikemaster and the overseers and the other landholders! That's on account of the high water!"

When I entered, I saw about a dozen men sitting round a table that extended beneath the windows; a punch bowl stood upon it; and a particularly stately man seemed to dominate the party.

I bowed and asked if I might sit down with them, a favor which was readily granted.

"You had better keep watch here!" I said, turning to this man; "the weather outside is bad; there will be hard times for the dikes!"

"Surely," he replied, "but we here on the east side believe we are out of danger. Only over there on the other side it isn't safe; the dikes there are mostly made more after old patterns; our chief dike was made in the last century. We got chilly outside a while ago; and you," he added, "probably had the same experience. But we have to hold out a few hours longer here; we have reliable people outside, who report to us." And before I could give my order to the host, a steaming glass was pushed in front of me.

I soon found out that my pleasant neighbour was the dikemaster; we entered into conversation, and I began to tell him about my strange encounter on the dike. He grew attentive, and I noticed suddenly that all talk round about was silenced.

"The rider on the white horse," cried one of the company and a movement of fright stirred the others.

The dikemaster had risen.

"You don't need to be afraid," he spoke across the table, "that isn't meant for us only; in the year '17 it was meant for them too; may they be ready for the worst!"

Now a horror came over me.

"Pardon me!" I said. "What about this rider on the white horse?"

Apart from the others, behind the stove, a small, haggard man in a little worn black coat sat somewhat bent over; one of his shoulders seemed a little deformed. He had not taken part with a single word in the conversation of the others, but his eyes, fringed as they were with dark lashes, although the scanty hair on his head was grey, showed clearly that he was not sitting there to sleep.

Toward him the dikemaster pointed:

"Our schoolmaster," he said, raising his voice, "will be the one among us who can tell you that best—to be sure, only in his way, and not quite as accurately as my old house-keeper at home, Antje Vollmans, would manage to tell it."

"You are joking, dikemaster!" the somewhat feeble voice of the schoolmaster rose from behind the stove, "if you want to compare me to your silly dragon!"

"Yes, that's all right, schoolmaster!" replied the other, "but stories of that kind are supposed to be kept safest with dragons."

"Indeed!" said the little man, "in this we are not quite of the same opinion." And a superior smile flitted over his delicate face.

"You see," the dikemaster whispered in my ear, "he is still a little proud; in his youth he once studied theology and it was only because of an unhappy courtship that he stayed hanging about his home as schoolmaster."

The schoolmaster had meanwhile come forward from his corner by the stove and had sat down beside me at the long table.

"Come on! Tell the story, schoolmaster," cried some of the younger members of the party.

"Yes, indeed," said the old man, turning toward me. "I will gladly oblige you; but there is a good deal of superstition mixed in with it, and it is quite a feat to tell the story without it."

"I must beg you not to leave the superstition out," I replied. "You can trust me to sift the chaff from the wheat by myself!"

The old man looked at me with an appreciative smile.

Well, he said, in the middle of the last century, or rather, to be more exact, before and after the middle of that century, there was a dikemaster here who knew more about dikes and sluices than peasants and landowners usually do. But I suppose it was nevertheless not quite enough, for he had read little of what learned specialists had written about it; his knowledge, though he began in childhood, he had thought out all by himself. I dare say you have heard, sir, that the Frisians are good at arithmetic, and perhaps you have heard tell of our Hans Mommsen from Fahntoft, who was a peasant and yet could make chronometers, telescopes, and organs. Well, the father of this man who later became dikemaster was made out of this same stuff—to be sure, only a little. He had a few fens, where he planted turnips and beans and kept a cow grazing; once in a while in the fall and spring he also surveyed land, and in winter, when the northwest wind blew outside and shook his shutters, he sat in his room to scratch and prick with his instruments. The boy usually would sit by and look away from his primer or Bible to watch his father measure and calculate, and would thrust his hand into his blond hair. And one evening he asked the old man why something that he had written down had to be just so and could not be something different, and stated his own opinion about it. But his father, who did not know how to answer this, shook his head and said:

"That I cannot tell you; anyway it is so, and you are mistaken. If you want to know more, search for a book to-morrow in a box in our attic; someone whose name is Euclid has written it; that will tell you."

The next day the boy had run up to the attic and soon had found the book, for there were not many books in the house anyway, but his father laughed when he laid it in front of him on the table. It was a Dutch Euclid, and Dutch, although it was half German, neither of them understood.

"Yes, yes," he said, "this book belonged to my father; he understood it; is there no German Euclid up there?"

The boy, who spoke little, looked at his father quietly and said only: "May I keep it? There isn't any German one."

And when the old man nodded, he showed him a second half-torn little book.

"That too?" he asked again.

"Take them both!" said Tede Haien; "they won't be of much use of you."

But the second book was a little Dutch grammar, and as the winter was not over for a long while, by the time the gooseberries bloomed again in the garden it had helped the boy so far that he could almost entirely understand his Euclid, which at that time was much in vogue.

I know perfectly well, sir, the story teller interrupted himself, that this same incident is also told of Hans Mommsen, but before his birth our people here have told the same of Hauke Haien—that was the name of the boy. You know well enough that as soon as a greater man has come, everything is heaped on him that his predecessor has done before him, either seriously or in fun.

When the old man saw that the boy had no sense for cows or sheep and scarcely noticed when the beans were in bloom, which is the joy of every marshman, and when he considered that his little place might be kept up by a farmer and a boy, but not by a half-scholar and a hired man, inasmuch as he himself had not been over-prosperous, he sent his big boy to the dike, where he had to cart earth from Easter until Martinmas. "That will cure him of his Euclid," he said to himself.

And the boy carted; but his Euclid he always had with him in his pocket, and when the workmen ate their breakfast or lunch, he sat on his upturned wheelbarrow with the book in his hand. In autumn, when the tide rose higher netimes work had to be stopped, he did not go home with the others, but stayed and sat with his hands clasped over his knees on the seaward slope of the dike, and for hours watched the sombre waves of the North Sea beat always higher and higher against the grass-grown scar of the dike. Not until the water washed over his feet and the foam sprayed his face did he move a few feet higher, only to stay and sit on. He did not hear the splash of the water, or the scream of the gulls or strand birds that flew round him and almost grazed him with their wings, flashing their black eyes at his own; nor did he see how night spread over the wide wilderness of water. The only thing he saw was the edge of the surf, which at high tide was again and again hitting the same place with hard blows and before his very eyes washing away the grassy scar of the steep dike.

After staring a long time, he would nod his head slowly and, without looking up, draw a curved line in the air, as if he could in this way give the dike a gentler slope. When it grew so dark that all earthly things vanished from his sight and only the surf roared in his ears, then he got up and marched home half drenched.

One night when he came in this state into the room where his father was polishing his surveying instruments, the latter started. "What have you been doing out there?" he cried. "You might have drowned; the waters are biting into the dike to-day."

Hauke looked at him stubbornly.

"Don't you hear me? I say, you might have drowned!"

"Yes," said Hauke, "but I'm not drowned!"

"No," the old man answered after a while and looked into his face absently—"not this time."

"But," Hauke returned, "our dikes aren't worth anything."

"What's that, boy?"

"The dikes, I say."

"What about the dikes?"

"They're no good, father," replied Hauke.

The old man laughed in his face. "What's the matter with you, boy? I suppose you are the prodigy from Lübeck."

But the boy would not be put down. "The waterside is too steep," he said; "if it happens some day as it has happened before, we can drown here behind the dike too."

The old man pulled his tobacco out of his pocket, twisted off a piece and pushed it behind his teeth. "And how many loads have you pushed to-day?" he asked angrily, for he saw that the boy's work on the dike had not been able to chase away his brainwork.

The Rider on the White Horse

"I don't know, father," said the boy; "about as many as the others did, perhaps half a dozen more; but—the dikes have got to be changed!"

"Well," said the old man with a short laugh, "perhaps you can manage to be made dikemaster; then you can change them."

"Yes, father," replied the boy.

The old man looked at him and swallowed a few times, then he walked out of the door. He did not know what to say to the boy.

Even when, at the end of October, the work on the dike was over, his walk northward to the farm was the best entertainment for Hauke Haien. He looked forward to All Saints' Day, the time when the equinoctial storms were wont to rage—a day on which we say that Friesland has a good right to mourn—just as children nowadays look forward to Christmas. When an early flood was coming, one could be sure that in spite of storm and bad weather, he would be lying all alone far out on the dike; and when the gulls chattered, when the waters pounded against the dike and as they rolled back swept big pieces of the grass cover with them into the sea, then one could have heard Hauke's furious laughter.

"You aren't good for anything!" he cried out into the noise. "Just as the people are no good!" And at last, often in darkness, he trotted home from the wide water along the dike, until his tall figure had reached the low door under his father's thatch roof and slipped into the little room.

Sometimes he had brought home a handful of clay; then he sat down beside the old man, who now humoured him, and by the light of the thin tallow candle he kneaded all sorts of dike models, laid them in a flat dish with water and tried to imitate the washing away by the waves; or he took his slate and drew the profiles of the dikes toward the waterside as he thought they ought to be.

He had no idea of keeping up intercourse with his schoolmates; it seemed, too, as if they did not care for this dreamer. When winter had come again and the frost had appeared, he wandered still farther out on the dike to points he had never reached before, until the boundless ice-covered sand flats lay before him.

During the continuous frost in February, dead bodies were found washed ashore; they had lain on the frozen sand flats by the open sea. A young woman who had been present when they had taken the bodies into the village, stood talking fluently with old Haien.

"Don't you believe that they looked like people!" she cried; "no, like sea devils! Heads as big as this," and she touched together the tips of her outspread and outstretched hands, "coal-black and shiny, like newly baked

ad nibbled them, and the children screamed when they
daien this was nothing new.

ney have floated in the water since November!" he said

e stood by in silence, but as soon as he could, he sneaked out on the
e; nobody knew whether he wanted to look for more dead, or if he was
drawn to the places now deserted by the horror that still clung to them. He
ran on and on, until he stood alone in the solitary waste, where only the
winds blew over the dike where there was nothing but the wailing voices of
the great birds that shot by swiftly. To his left was the wide empty marshland, on the other side the endless beach with its sand flats now glistening
with ice; it seemed as if the whole world lay in a white death.

Hauke remained standing on the dike, and his sharp eyes gazed far away.
There was no sign of the dead; but when the invisible streams on the sand
flats found their way beneath the ice, it rose and sank in streamlike lines.

He ran home, but on one of the next nights he was out there again. In
places the ice had now split; smoke-clouds seemed to rise out of the cracks,
and over the whole sand-stretch a net of steam and mist seemed to be spun,
which at evening mingled strangely with the twilight. Hauke stared at it with
fixed eyes, for in the mist dark figures were walking up and down that
seemed to him as big as human beings. Far off he saw them promenade back
and forth by the steaming fissures, dignified, but with strange, frightening
gestures, with long necks and noses. All at once, they began to jump up and
down like fools, uncannily, the big ones over the little ones, the little ones
over the big ones—then they spread out and lost all shape.

"What do they want? Are they ghosts of the drowned?" thought Hauke.
"Hallo!" he screamed out aloud into the night; but they did not heed his cry
and kept on with their strange antics.

Then the terrible Norwegian sea spectres came to his mind, that an old
captain had once told him about, who bore stubby bunches of sea grass on
their necks instead of heads. He did not run away, however, but dug the heels
of his boots faster into the clay of the dike and rigidly watched the farcical
riot that was kept up before his eyes in the falling dusk. "Are you here in our
parts too?" he said in a hard voice. "You shall not chase me away!"

Not until darkness covered all things did he walk home with stiff, slow
steps. But behind him he seemed to hear the rustling of wings and resounding
screams. He did not look round, neither did he walk faster, and it was late
when he came home. Yet he is said to have told neither his father nor anyone
else about it. But many years after he took his feeble-minded little girl, with
whom the Lord later had burdened him, out on the dike with him at the same

time of day and year, and the same riot is said to have appeared then out on the sand flats. But he told her not to be afraid, that these things were only the herons and crows, that seemed so big and horrible, and that they were getting fish out of the open cracks.

God knows, the schoolmaster interrupted himself, there are all sorts of things on earth that could confuse a Christian heart, but Hauke was neither a fool nor a blockhead.

As I made no response, he wanted to go on. But among the other guests, who till now had listened without making a sound, only filling the low room more and more thickly with tobacco smoke, there arose a sudden stir. First one, then another, then all turned toward the window. Outside, as one could see through the uncurtained glass, the storm was driving the clouds, and light and dark were chasing one another; but it seemed to me too as if I had seen the haggard rider whiz by on his white horse.

"Wait a little, schoolmaster," said the dikemaster in a low voice.

"You don't need to be afraid, dikemaster," laughed the little narrator. "I have not slandered him and have no reason to do so"—and he looked up at him with his small clever eyes.

"All right," said the other. "Let your glass be filled again!" And when that had been done and the listeners, most of them with rather anxious faces, had turned to him again, he went on with his story:

Living thus by himself and liking best to associate only with sand and water and with scenes of solitude, Hauke grew into a long lean fellow. It was a year after his confirmation that his life was suddenly changed, and this came about through the old white Angora cat which old Trin Jans's son, who later perished at sea, had brought her on his return from a voyage to Spain. Trin lived a good way out on the dike in a little hut, and when the old woman did her chores in the house, this monster of a cat used to sit in front of the house door and blink into the summer day and at the peewits that flew past. When Hauke went by, the cat mewed at him and Hauke nodded; both knew how each felt toward the other.

Now it was spring and Hauke, as he was accustomed to do, often lay out on the dike, already farther out near the water, between beach pinks and the fragrant sea-wormwood, and let the strong sun shine on him. He had gathered his pockets full of pebbles up on the higher land the day before, and when at low tide the sand flats were laid bare and the little gay strand snipes whisked across them screaming, he quickly pulled out a stone and threw it after the birds. He had practiced this from earliest childhood on, and usually one of the birds remained lying on the ground; but often it was impossible to get at it. Hauke had sometimes thought of taking the cat with him and training him as a retriever. But there were hard places here and there on the sand; in that case he ran and got his prey himself. On his way back, if the cat was still sitting in front of the house door, the animal would utter piercing cries of uncontrollable greed until Hauke threw him one of the birds he had killed.

To-day when he walked home, carrying his jacket on his shoulder, he was taking home only one unknown bird, but that seemed to have wings of gay silk and metal; and the cat mewed as usual when he saw him coming. But this time Hauke did not want to give up his prey—it may have been an ice bird—and he paid no attention to the greed of the animal. "Wait your turn!" he called to him. "To-day for me, to-morrow for you; this is no food for a cat!"

As the cat came carefully sneaking along, Hauke stood and looked at it: the bird was hanging from his hand, and the cat stood still with its paw raised. But it seemed that the young man did not know his cat friend too well, for, while he had turned his back on it and was just going on his way, he felt that with a sudden jerk his booty was torn from him, and at the same time a sharp claw cut into his flesh. A rage like that of a beast of prey shot into the young man's blood; wildly he stretched out his arm and in a flash had clutched the robber by his neck. With his fist he held the powerful animal high up and choked it until its eyes bulged out among its rough hairs, not heeding that the strong hind paws were tearing his flesh. "Hello!" he shouted, and clutched him still more tightly; "let's see which of us two can stand it the longest!"

Suddenly the hind legs of the big cat fell languidly down, and Hauke walked back a few steps and threw it against the hut of the old woman. As it did not stir, he turned round and continued his way home.

But the Angora cat was the only treasure of her mistress; he was her companion and the only thing that her son, the sailor, had left her after he had met with sudden death here on the coast when he had wanted to help his mother by fishing in the storm. Hauke had scarcely walked on a hundred steps, while he caught the blood from his wounds on a cloth, when he heard a shrill howling and screaming from the hut. He turned round and, in front of it, saw the old woman lying on the ground; her grey hair was flying in the wind round her red head scarf.

"Dead!" she cried; "dead!" and raised her lean arm threateningly against him: "A curse on you! You have killed her, you good for nothing vagabond; you weren't good enough to brush her tail!" She threw herself upon the animal and with her apron she tenderly wiped off the blood that was still running from its nose and mouth; then she began her screaming again.

"When will you be done?" Hauke cried to her. "Then let me tell you, I'll get you a cat that will be satisfied with the blood of mice and rats!"

Then he went on his way, apparently no longer concerned with anything. But the dead cat must have caused some confusion in his head, for when he came to the village, he passed by his father's house and the others and walked on a good distance toward the south on the dike toward the city.

Meanwhile Trin Jans, too, wandered on the dike in the same direction. In her arms she bore a burden wrapped in an old blue checkered pillowcase, and clasped it carefully as if it were a child; her grey hair fluttered in the light spring wind. "What are you lugging there, Trina?" asked a peasant who met her. "More than your house and farm," replied the old woman, and walked on eagerly. When she came near the house of old Haien, which lay below, she walked down to the houses along the "akt," as we call the cattle and foot paths that lead slantingly up and down the side of the dike.

Old Tede Haien was just standing in front of his door, looking at the weather. "Well, Trin!" he said, when she stood panting in front of him and dug her crutch into the ground, "What are you bringing us in your bag?"

"First let me into the room, Tede Haien! Then you shall see!" and her eyes looked at him with a strange gleam.

"Well, come along!" said the old man. What did he care about the eyes of the stupid woman!

When both had entered, she went on: "Take that old tobacco box and those writing things from the table. What do you always have to write for, anyway? All right; and now wipe it clean!"

And the old man, who was almost growing curious, did everything just as she said. Then she took the blue pillow-case at both ends and emptied the carcass of the big cat out on the table. "There she is!" she cried; "your Hauke has killed her!" Thereupon she began to cry bitterly; she stroked the thick fur of the dead animal, laid its paws together, bent her long nose over its head and whispered incomprehensible words of tenderness into its ears.

Tede Haien watched this. "Is that so," he said; "Hauke has killed her?"

He did not know what to do with the howling woman.

She nodded at him grimly. "Yes, yes, God knows, that's what he has done," and she wiped the tears from her eyes with her hand, crippled by rheumatism. "No child, no live thing any more!" she complained. "And you know yourself how it is after All Saints' Day, when we old people feel our legs shiver at night in bed, and instead of sleeping we hear the northwest wind rattle against the shutters. I don't like to hear it. Tede Haien, it comes from where my boy sank to death in the quicksand!"

Tede Haien nodded, and the old woman stroked the fur of her dead cat. "But this one here," she began again, "when I would sit by my spinning-wheel, there she would sit with me and spin too and look at me with her green eyes! And when I grew cold and crept into my bed—then it wasn't long before she jumped up to me and lay down on my chilly legs, and we both slept as warmly together as if I still had my young sweetheart in bed!"

The old woman, as if she were waiting for his assent to this remembrance, looked with her gleaming eyes at the old man standing beside her at the table. Tede Haien, however, said thoughtfully: "I know a way out for you, Trin Jans," and he went to his strong box and took a silver coin out of the drawer. "You say that Hauke has robbed your animal of life, and I know you don't lie; but here is a crown piece from the time of Christian IV; go and buy a tanned lamb-skin with it for your cold legs! And when our cat has kittens, you may pick out the biggest of them; both together, I suppose, will make up for an Angora cat feeble from old age! Take your beast and, if you want to, take it to the tanner in town, but keep your mouth shut and don't tell that it has lain on my honest table."

During this speech the woman had already snatched the crown and stowed it away in a little bag that she carried under her skirts, then she tucked the cat back into the pillowcase, wiped the bloodstains from the table with her apron, and stalked out of the door. "Don't you forget the young cat!" she called back.

After a while, when old Haien was walking up and down in the narrow little room, Hauke stepped in and tossed his bright bird on to the table. But when he saw the still recognizable bloodstain on the clean white top, he asked as if by the way: "What's that?"

His father stood still. "That's blood that you have spilled!"

The young man flushed hotly. "Why, has Trin Jans been here with her cat?"

The old man nodded: "Why did you kill it?"

Hauke uncovered his bleeding arm. "That's why," he said. "She had torn my bird away from me!"

Thereupon the old man said nothing. For a time he began to walk up and down, then he stood still in front of the young man and looked at him for a while almost absently.

"This affair with the cat I have made all right," he said, "but look, Hauke, this place is too small; two people can't stay on it—it is time you got a job!"

"Yes, father," replied Hauke; "I have been thinking something of the sort myself."

"Why?" asked the old man.

"Well, one gets wild inside unless one can let it out on a decent piece of work!"

"Is that so?" said the old man, "and that's why you have killed the Angora cat? That might easily lead to something worse!"

"You may be right, father, but the dikemaster has discharged his farmhand; I could do that work all right!"

The old man began to walk up and down, and meanwhile spat out the black tobacco. "The dikemaster is a blockhead, as stupid as a goose! He is dikemaster only because his father and grandfather have been the same, and on account of his twenty-nine fens. Round Martinmas, when the dike and sluice bills have to be settled, then he feeds the schoolmaster on roast goose and mead and wheat buns, and sits by and nods while the other man runs down the columns of figures with his pen, and says: 'Yes, yes, schoolmaster, God reward you! How finely you calculate!' But when the schoolmaster can't or won't, then he has to go at it himself and sits scribbling and striking out again, his big stupid head growing red and hot, his eyes bulging out like glass balls, as if his little bit of sense wanted to get out that way."

The young man stood up straight in front of his father and marveled at his talking; he had never heard him speak like that. "Yes, God knows," he said, "no doubt he is stupid, but his daughter Elke, she can calculate!"

The old man looked at him sharply.

"Hallo, Hauke," he exclaimed "what do you know about Elke Volkerts?"

"Nothing, father; only the schoolmaster has told me?"

The old man made no reply; he only pushed his piece of tobacco thoughtfully from one cheek into the other. "And you think," he said, "that you can help in the counting there too."

"Oh, yes, father, that would work all right," the son replied, and there was a serious twitching about his mouth.

The old man shook his head: "Well, go if you like; go and try your luck!"

"Thanks, father!" said Hauke, and climbed up to his sleeping place in the garret. There he sat down on the edge of the bed and pondered why his father had shouted at him so when he had mentioned Elke Volkerts. To be sure, he knew the slender, eighteen-year-old girl with the tanned, narrow face and the dark eyebrows that ran into each other over the stubborn eyes and the slender nose; but he had scarcely spoken a word to her. Now, if he should go to old Tede Volkerts, he would look at her more and see what there was about the girl. Right off he wanted to go, so that no one else could snatch the position away from him—it was now scarcely evening. And so he put on his Sunday coat and his best boots and started out in good spirits.

The long rambling house of the dikemaster was visible from afar because of the high mound on which it stood, and especially because of the highest tree in the village, a mighty ash. The grandfather of the present dikemaster, the first of the line, had in his youth planted an ash to the east of the house door; but the first two had died, and so he had planted a third on his wedding morning, which was still murmuring as if of old times in the increasing wind with its crown of foliage that was growing mightier and mightier.

When, after a while, tall, lank Hauke climbed up the hill which was planted on both sides with beets and cabbage, he saw the daughter of the owner standing beside the low house door. One of her somewhat thin arms was hanging down languidly, the other seemed to be grasping behind her back at one of the iron rings which were fastened to the wall on either side of the door, so that anyone who rode to the house could use them to hitch his horse. From there the young girl seemed to be gazing over the dike at the sea, where on this calm evening the sun was just sinking into the water and at the same time gilding the dark-skinned maiden with its last golden glow.

Hauke climbed up the hill a little more slowly, and thought to himself: "She doesn't look so dull this way!" Then he was at the top. "Good evening to you!" he said, stepping up to her. "What are you looking at with your big eyes, Miss Elke?"

"I'm looking," she replied, "at something that goes on here every night, but can't be seen here every night." She let the ring drop from her hand, so that it fell against the wall with a clang. "What do you want, Hauke Haien?" she asked.

"Something that I hope you don't mind," he said. "Your father has just discharged his hired man; so I thought I would take a job with you."

She glanced at him, up and down: "You are still rather lanky, Hauke!" she said, "but two steady eyes serve us better than two steady arms!" At the same time she looked at him almost sombrely, but Hauke bravely withstood her gaze. "Come on, then," she continued. "The master is in his room; let's go inside."

The next day Tede Haien stepped with his son into the spacious room of the dikemaster. The walls were covered with glazed tiles on which the visitor could enjoy her a ship with sails unfurled or an angler on the shore, there a cow that lay chewing in front of a peasant's house. This durable wall-covering was interrupted by an alcove-bed with doors now closed, and a cupboard which showed all kinds of china and silver dishes through glass doors. Beside the door to the "best room" a Dutch clock was set into the wall behind a pane of glass.

The stout, somewhat apoplectic master of the house sat at the end of the well-scrubbed, shining table in an armchair with a bright-coloured cushion. He had folded his hands across his stomach, and was staring contentedly with his round eyes at the skeleton of a fat duck; knife and fork were resting in front of him on his plate.

"Good day, dikemaster!" said Haien, and the gentleman thus addressed slowly turned his head and eyes toward him.

"You here, Tede?" he replied, and the devoured fat duck had left its mark on his voice. "Sit down; it is quite a walk from your place over here!"

"I have come, dikemaster," said Tede Haien, while he sat down opposite the other in a corner on the bench that ran along the wall. "You have had trouble with your hired man and have agreed with my boy to put him in his place!"

The dikemaster nodded: "Yes, yes, Tede; but—what do you mean by trouble? We people of the marshes, thank goodness, have something to take against troubles!"—and he took the knife before him and patted the skeleton of the poor duck almost affectionately. "This was my pet bird," he added laughing smugly; "he fed out of my hand!"

"I thought," said old Haien, not hearing the last remark, "the boy had done harm in your stable."

"Harm? Yes, Tede; surely harm enough! That fat clown hadn't watered the calves; but he lay drunk on the hayloft, and the beasts bellowed all night with thirst, so that I had to make up my lost sleep till noon; that's not the way a farm can go on!"

"No, dikemaster; but there is no danger of that happening with my boy."

Hauke stood, his hands in his pockets, by the door-post, and had thrown back his head and was studying the window frames opposite him.

The dikemaster had raised his eyes and nodded toward him: "No, no, Tede,"—and now he nodded at the old man too; "your Hauke won't disturb my night's rest; the schoolmaster has told me before that he would rather sit with his slate and do arithmetic than with a glass of whiskey."

Hauke did not hear this encouragement, for Elke had stepped into the room and with her light hand took out the remnants from the table, meanwhile glancing at him carelessly with her dark eyes. Then his glances fell on her too. "By my faith," he said to himself, "she doesn't look so dull now either!"

The girl had left the room. "You know, Tede," the dikemaster began again, "the Lord has not granted me a son!"

"Yes, dikemaster, but don't let that worry you," replied the other, "for they say that in the third generation the brains of a family run out; your grandfather, we all remember, was a man who protected the land!"

The dikemaster, after some pondering, looked quite puzzled: "How do you mean, Tede Haien?" he said and sat up in his armchair; "I am in the third generation myself!"

"Oh, indeed! Never mind, dikemaster; that's just what people say!" And the lean Tede Haien looked at the old dignitary with rather mischievous eyes.

The latter, however, spoke unconcerned: "You mustn't let old women get nonsense like that into your head, Tede Haien; you don't know my daughter yet—she can calculate three times better than I can! I only wanted to say, your Hauke will be able to make some profit outside of his field work in my room with pen and pencil, and that will do him no harm."

"Yes, yes, dikemaster, he can do that; there you are perfectly right;" said old Haien and then began to demand some privileges with the contract which his son had not thought of the night before. For instance, the latter should receive, besides his linen shirts, eight pair of woollen stockings in addition to his wages; also he wanted to have his son's help at his own work for eight days in spring—and more of the sort. But the dikemaster agreed to everything; Hauke Haien appeared to him just the right servant.

"Well, God help you, my boy," said the old man, when they had just left the house, "if that man is to make the world clear to you!"

But Hauke replied calmly: "Never mind, father; everything will turn out all right."

Hauke had not been wrong in his judgment. The world, or what the world meant to him, grew clearer to his mind, the longer he stayed in this house—perhaps all the more, the less he was helped by a wiser insight and the more, he had to depend on his own powers with which he had from the beginning helped himself. There was someone in the house, however, whom he did not seem to suit; that was Ole Peters, the head man, a good worker and a great talker. The former lazy and stupid but stocky hired man had been more to his liking, whose back he could load calmly with a barrel of oats and whom he could knock about to his heart's content. Hauke, who was still more silent, but who surpassed him mentally, he could not treat in the same way; Hauke had too strange a way of looking at him. Nevertheless he managed to pick out tasks which might have been dangerous for the young man's yet undeveloped body; and when the head man would say: "You ought to have seen fat Nick, he could do it without any trouble at all," then Hauke would work with all his might and finish the task, although with difficulty. It was lucky for him that Elke usually could hinder this, either by herself or through her father. One may ask what it is that binds people who are complete strangers to each other; perhaps—well, they were both born arithmeticians, and the girl could not bear to see her comrade ruined by rough work.

The Rider on the White Horse

The conflict between head man and second man did not grow les[s] after Martinmas the different dike bills came in for revision.

It happened on a May evening, but the weather was like November; inside the house one could hear the surf roar outside from behind the dike.

"Hey, Hauke," said the master of the house, "come in; now is your chance to show if you can do arithmetic!"

"Master," Hauke replied; "I'm supposed to feed the young cattle first."

"Elke!" called the dikemaster; "where are you, Elke? Go and tell Ole to feed the young cattle; I want Hauke to calculate!"

So Elke hurried into the stable and gave the order to the head man who was just busy hanging the harness used during the day back in place.

Ole Peters whipped the post beside which he had been busying himself with a bridle, as if he wanted to beat it to pieces: "The devil take that cursed scribbler!"

She heard these words even before she had closed the stable door again.

"Well?" asked the old man, as she stepped into the room.

"Ole was willing to do it," said his daughter, biting her lips a little, and sat down opposite Hauke on one of the roughly carved chairs which in those days were still made at home on winter evenings. Out of a drawer she had taken a white stocking with a red bird pattern on it, which she was now knitting; the long-legged creatures might have represented herons or storks. Hauke sat opposite her, deep in his arithmetic; the dikemaster himself rested in his armchair and blinked sleepily at Hauke's pen. On the table, as always in the house of the dikemaster, two tallow candles were burning, and behind the windows with their leaden frames the shutters were closed and fastened from within; now the wind could bang against them as hard as it liked. Once in a while Hauke raised his head and glanced for a moment at the bird stockings or at the narrow, calm face of the girl.

Suddenly from the armchair there rose a loud snore, and a glance and smile flew back and forth between the two young people; gradually the breathing grew more quiet, and one could easily talk a little—only Hauke did not know about what.

But when she raised her knitting and the birds appeared in their whole length, he whispered across the table: "Where have you learned that, Elke?"

"Learned what?" the girl returned.

"This bird knitting?" said Hauke.

"This? From Trin Jans out there on the dike; she can do all sorts of things. She was servant here to my grandfather a long time ago."

"At that time I don't suppose you were born?" said Hauke.

"I think not; but she has often come to the house since then."

"Does she like birds?" asked Hauke; "I thought only cats were for her."

Elke shook her head: "Why, she raises ducks and sells them; but last spring, when you had killed her Angora cat, the rats got into the pen at the back of the house and made mischief; now she wants to build herself another in front of the house."

"Is that so?" said Hauke and whistled low through his teeth, "that's why she dragged mud and stones from the upper land. But then she will get on to the inland road; has she a grant?"

"I don't know," said Elke. But he had spoken the last word so loud that the dikemaster started out of his slumber.

"What grant?" he asked and looked almost wildly from one to the other. "What about the grant?"

But when Hauke had explained the matter to him, he slapped the young man's shoulder, laughing: "Oh, well, the inland road is broad enough; God help the dikemaster if he has to worry about duck pens!"

It weighed on Hauke's heart that he should have delivered the old woman and her ducks over to the rats, but he allowed himself to be quieted by this objection. "But, master," he began again, "it might be good for some people to be prodded a little, and if you don't want to go after them yourself, why don't you prod the overseers who ought to look out for order on the dike?"

"How—what is the boy saying?" and the dikemaster sat up straight, and Elke let her fancy stocking sink down and turned an ear toward Hauke.

"Yes, master," Hauke went on, "you have already gone round on your spring inspection; but just the same Peter Jansen hasn't weeded his lot to this day; and in summer the goldfinches will play round the red thistles as gaily as ever. And near by—I don't know to whom it belongs—there is a hole like a cradle on the outer side of the dike; when the weather is good it is always full of little children that roll in it; but—God save us from high water!"

The eyes of the old dikemaster had grown bigger and bigger.

"And then—"said Hauke again.

"Then what more, boy?" asked the dikemaster; "haven't you finished yet?" and it seemed as if he had already had too much of his second man's speech.

"Yes; then, master," Hauke went on; "you know that fat Vollina, the daughter of the overseer Harder, who always fetches her father's horse from the fen—well, as soon as she sits with her round legs on the old yellow mare—Get up!—why, then every time she goes diagonally up the slope of the dike!"

Hauke did not notice until now that Elke had fixed her intelligent eyes on him and was gently shaking her head.

He was silent, but a bang on the table from the old man's fist thundered in his ears. "Confound it!" he cried, and Hauke was almost frightened by the bear's voice that suddenly broke out: "to the fens! Note down that fat creature in the fens, Hauke! That girl caught three of my young ducks last summer! Yes, yes, put it down," he repeated, when Hauke hesitated; "I even believe there were four!"

"Oh, father," said Elke, "wasn't it an otter that took the ducks?"

"A big otter!" cried the old man, panting; I guess I can tell the fat Vollina and an otter apart! No, no, four ducks, Hauke—but as for the rest of what you have been chattering—last spring the dikemaster general and I, after we had breakfasted together at my house, drove by your weeds and your cradle-hole and yet couldn't see anything. But you two," and he nodded a few times significantly at Hauke and his daughter, "you can thank God that you are no dikemaster! Two eyes are all one has, and one is supposed to look with a hundred. Take the bills for the straw coverings, Hauke, and look them over; those rascals do keep their accounts in such a shiftless way!"

Then he leaned back in his chair again, moved his heavy body a few times and soon gave himself over to care-free slumber.

The same thing was repeated on many an evening. Hauke had sharp eyes, and when they sat together, he did not neglect to call the old man's attention to one or the other violation or omission in dike matters, and as the latter could not always keep his eyes closed, unawares the management acquired a greater efficiency and those who in other times had gone on sinning in their old, careless ways and now, as it were, unexpectedly felt their mischievous or lazy fingers slapped, looked round indignantly and with astonishment to see whence these slaps had come. And Ole, the head man, did not hesitate to spread the information and in this way to rouse indignation among these people against Hauke and his father, who had to bear part of the guilt. The others, however, who were not affected or who were not concerned with the matter, laughed and rejoiced to see that the young man had at last got the old man going a bit. "It's only too bad," they said, "that the young fellow hasn't enough ground under his feet; else he might make a dikemaster of the kind we used to have—but those few acres of his old man wouldn't do, after all!"

Next autumn, when the inspector and the dikemaster general came for the inspection, he looked at old Tede Volkerts from top to toe, while the latter was urging him to sit down to lunch.

"I tell you, dikemaster," he said, "I was thinking—you have actually grown ten years younger. You have set my blood coursing with all your proposals; if only we can get down with all that to-day!"

"Oh, we shall, we shall, your Honor," replied the old man with a smirk; "the roast goose over there will give us strength! Yes, thank God, I am still always well and brisk!" He looked round the room to make sure that Hauke was not about; then he added with calm dignity: "And so I hope I may fulfill the duties of my office a few more blessed years."

"And to this, my dear dikemaster," returned his superior, "we want to drink this glass together."

Elke who had looked after the lunch laughed to herself as she left the room just when the glasses were clicking. Then she took a dish of scraps from the kitchen and walked through the stable to give them to the poultry in front of the outside door. In the stable stood Hauke Haien and with his pitch-fork put hay into the racks of the cows that had to be brought up here so early because of the bad weather. But when he saw the girl come, he stuck the pitchfork into the ground. "Well, Elke!" he said.

She stood still and nodded at him: "All right, Hauke—but you should have been in there!"

"Do you think so? Why, Elke?"

"The dikemaster general has praised the master!"

"The master? What has that to do with me?"

"No, I mean, he has praised the dikemaster!"

The young man's face was flushed crimson: "I know very well," he said, "what you are driving at."

"Don't blush, Hauke; it was really you whom the dikemaster general praised!"

Hauke looked at her with a half smile. "You too, Elke!" he said.

But she shook her head: "No, Hauke; when I was helper alone, we got no praise. And then, I can only do arithmetic; but you see everything outdoors that the dikemaster is supposed to see for himself. You have cut me out!"

"That isn't what I intended—least of all you!" said Hauke timidly, and he pushed aside the head of a cow. "Come, Redskin, don't swallow my pitchfork, you'll get all you want!"

"Don't think that I'm sorry, Hauke;" said the girl after thinking a little while; "that really is a man's business."

Then Hauke stretched out his arm toward her. "Elke, give me your hand, so that I can be sure."

Beneath her dark brows a deep crimson flushed the girl's face. "Why? I'm not lying!" she cried.

Hauke wanted to reply; but she had already left the stable, and he stood with his pitchfork in his hand and heard only the cackling and crowing of the ducks and the hens round her outside.

In the January of Hauke's third year of service a winter festival was to be held—"Eisboseln" they call it here. The winds had been calm on the coast and steady frost had covered all the ditches between the fens with a solid, even, crystal surface, so that the marked-off strips of land offered a wide field for the throwing at a goal of little wooden balls filled with lead. Day in, day out, a light northeast wind was blowing: everything had been prepared. The people from the higher land, inhabitants of the village that lay eastward above the marshes, who had won last year, had been challenged to a match and had accepted. From either side nine players had been picked. The umpire and the score-keepers had been chosen. The latter, who had to discuss a doubtful throw whenever a difference of opinion came up, were always chosen from among people who knew how to place their own case in the best possible light, preferably young fellows who not only had good common sense but also a ready tongue. Among these was, above all, Ole Peters, the head man of the dikemaster. "Throw away like devils!" he said; "I'll do the talking for nothing!"

Toward evening on the day before the holiday a number of throwers had appeared in the side room of the parish inn up on the higher land, in order to decide about accepting some men who had applied in the last moment. Hauke Haien was among these. At first he had not wanted to take part, although he was well aware of having arms skilled in throwing; but he was afraid that he might be rejected by Ole Peters who had a post of honor in the game, and he wanted to spare himself this defeat. But Elke had made him change his mind at the eleventh hour. "He won't dare, Hauke," she had said; "he is the son of a day laborer; your father has his cow and horse and is the cleverest man in the village."

"But if he should manage to, after all?"

Half smiling she looked at him with her dark eyes. "Then he'll get left," she said, "in the evening, when he wants to dance with his master's daughter." Then Hauke had nodded to her with spirit.

Now the young men who still hoped to be taken into the game stood shivering and stamping outside the parish inn and looked up at the top of the stone church tower which stood beside the tavern. The pastor's pigeons which during the summer found their food on the fields of the village were just returning from the farmyards and barns of the peasants, where they had pecked their grain, and were disappearing into their nests underneath the shingles of the tower. In the west, over the sea, there was a glowing sunset.

"We'll have good weather to-morrow," said one of the young fellows, and began to wander up and down excitedly; "but cold—cold." Another man, when he saw no more pigeons flying, walked into the house and stood listening beside the door of the room in which a lively babble was now sounding. The second man of the dikemaster, too, had stepped up beside him. "Listen, Hauke," he said to the latter; "now they are making all this noise about you." And clearly one could hear from inside Ole Peters's grating voice: "Underlings and boys don't belong here!"

"Come," whispered the other man and tried to pull Hauke by his sleeve to the door of the room, "here you can learn how high they value you."

But Hauke tore himself away and went to the front of the house again: "They haven't barred us out so that we should hear," he called back.

Before the house stood the third of the applicants. "I'm afraid there's a hitch in this business for me," he called to Hauke; "I'm barely eighteen years old; if they only won't ask for my birth certificate! Your head man, Hauke, will get you out of your fix, all right!"

"Yes, out!" growled Hauke and kicked a stone across the road; "but not in!"

The noise in the room was growing louder; then gradually there was calm. Those outside could again hear the gentle northeast wind that broke against the point of the church steeple. The man who listened joined them. "Whom did they take in there?" asked the eighteen-year-old one.

"Him!" said the other, and pointed to Hauke; "Ole Peters wanted to make him out as a boy; but the others shouted against it.—'And his father has cattle and land,' said Jess Hansen.—'Yes, land,' cried Ole Peters, 'land that one can cart away on thirteen wheelbarrows!' Last came Ole Hensen: 'Keep still!' he cried; 'I'll make things clear: tell me, who is the first man in the village?'—Then all kept mum and seemed to be thinking. Then a voice said: 'I should say it was the dikemaster!'—'And who is the dikemaster?' cried Ole Hensen again; 'but now think twice!'—Then somebody began to laugh quietly, and then someone else too, and so on till there was nothing but loud laughter in the room.—'Well, then call him,' said Ole Hensen; 'you don't want to keep the dikemaster out in the cold!'—I believe they're still laughing; but Ole Peters's voice could not be heard any more!" Thus the young fellow ended his account.

Almost in the same instant the door of the room inside the house was opened suddenly and out into the cold night sounded loud and merry cries of "Hauke! Hauke Haien!"

Then Hauke marched into the house and never could hear the rest of the story of who was the dikemaster; meanwhile no one has found out what was going on in his head.

After a while, when he approached the house of his employers, he saw Elke standing by the fence below, where the ascent began; the moonlight was shimmering over the measureless white frosted pasture.

"You are standing here, Elke?" he asked.

She only nodded: "What happened?" she said; "has he dared?"

"What wouldn't he—?"

"Well, and—?"

"Yes, Elke; I'm allowed to try it to-morrow!"

"Good night, Hauke!" And she fled up the slope and vanished into the house.

Slowly he followed her.

Next afternoon on the wide pasture that extended in the east along the land side of the dike, one could see a dark crowd. Now it would stand motionless, now move gradually on, down from the long and low houses lying behind it, as soon as a wooden ball had twice shot forth from it over the ground now freed by the bright sun from frost. The teams of the "Eisbosler" were in the middle, surrounded by old and young, by all who lived with them in these houses or up in those of the higher land—the older men in long coats, pensively smoking their short pipes, the women in shawls or jackets, some leading children by the hand or carrying them on their arms. From the frozen ditches, which were being crossed gradually, the pale light of the afternoon sun was gleaming through the sharp points of the sedges. It was keen frost, but the game went on uninterruptedly, and the eyes of all were again and again following the flying ball, for upon it depended the honor of the whole village for the day. The score-keepers of the two sides carried a white stick with an iron point for the home team, a black one of the same kind for the team of the people from the upper land. Where the ball ended its flight, the stick was driven into the frozen ground, accompanied, as it happened, either by silent approval or the derisive laughter of the opposing side; and he whose ball had first reached the goal, had won the game for his team.

Little was said by all these people; only when a capital throw had been made, a cry from the young men or women could be heard; sometimes, too, one of the old men would take his pipe out of his mouth and knock with it on the shoulder of the thrower with a few cheering words: "That was a good throw, said Zacharias, and threw his wife out of the door!" or: "That's the way your father threw, too; God bless him in eternity!" or some other friendly saying.

Hauke had no luck with his first throw: just as he was swinging his arm backward in order to hurl off the ball, a cloud sailed away which had covered the sun so that now its bright beams shot into his eyes; the throw was too short, the ball fell on a ditch and remained stuck in the ice.

"That doesn't count! That doesn't count! Hauke, once more!" called his partners.

But the score-keeper of the people from the high land protested against this: "It'll have to count; a throw is a throw!"

"Ole! Ole Peters!" cried the young folks of the marshes. "Where is Ole? Where the devil is he?"

But there he was: "Don't scream so! Does Hauke have to be patched up somewhere? I thought as much."

"Never mind! Hauke has to throw again; now show that your tongue is good for something!"

"Oh, it is all right!" cried Ole and stepped up to the scorekeeper of the other side and talked a lot of bosh. But the pointedness and sharpness of his usually so scintillating words were absent this time. Beside him stood the girl with the enigmatic eyebrows and looked at him sharply with angry glances; but she was not allowed to talk, for women had no say in the game.

"You are babbling nonsense," cried the other scorekeeper, "because you can't use any sense for this! Sun, moon and stars are alike for us all and always in the sky; the throw was awkward, and all awkward throws have to count!"

Thus they talked back and forth a little while, but the end of it was that, according to the decision of the umpire, Hauke was not allowed to repeat his throw.

"Come on!" called the people from the upper land, and their score-keeper pulled the black stick out of the ground, and the thrower came forward when his number was called and hurled the ball ahead. When the head man of the dikemaster wanted to watch the throw, he had to pass Elke Volkerts: "For whose sake have you left your brains at home to-day?" she whispered to him.

Then he looked at her almost grimly, and all joking was gone from his broad face. "For your sake," he said, "for you have forgotten yours too!"

"Go, go—I know you, Ole Peters!" the girl replied, drawing herself up straight. But he turned his head away and pretended not to have heard.

And the game and the black and white stick went on. When Hauke's turn to throw came again, his ball flew so far, that the goal, the great whitewashed barrel, came clearly in sight. He was now a solidly built young fellow, and mathematics and the art of throwing he had practised daily in his boyhood. "Why, Hauke!" there were cries from the crowd; "that was just as if the archangel Michael himself had thrown the ball!" An old woman with cake and brandy pushed her way through the crowd toward him; she poured out a glass for him and offered it to him: "Come," she said, "we want to be friends: this to-day is better than when you killed my cat!" When he looked at her, he recognised her as Trin Jans. "Thank you, old lady," he said; "but I don't drink that." He put his hand into his pocket and pressed a newly minted mark piece into her hand: "Take that and empty your glass yourself, Trin; and so we are friends!"

"You're right, Hauke!" replied the old woman, while she obeyed his instructions; "you're right; that's better for an old woman like me!"

"How are your ducks getting on" he called after her, when she had already started on her way with her basket; but she only shook her head, without turning round, and struck the air with her old hands. "Nothing, nothing, Hauke; there are too many rats in your ditches; God help me, but I've got to support myself some other way!" And so she pushed her way into the crowd and again offered her brandy and honey cake.

The sun had at last gone down behind the dike; in his stead rose a red violet glimmer; now and then black crows flew by and for moments looked gilded: evening had come. But on the fens the dark mass of people were moving still farther away from the already distant houses toward the barrel; an especially good throw would have to reach it now. The people of the marshes were having their turn: Hauke was to throw.

The chalky barrel showed white against the broad evening shadow that now fell from the dike across the plain.

"I guess you'll leave it to us this time," called one of the people of the upper land, for it was very close; they had the advantage of at least ten feet.

Hauke's lean figure was just stepping out of the crowd; the grey eyes in his long Frisian face were looking ahead at the barrel; in his hand which hung down he held the ball.

"I suppose the bird is too big for you," he heard Ole Peters's grating voice in this instant behind his ears; "shall we exchange it for a grey pot?"

Hauke turned round and looked at him with steady eyes: "I'm throwing for the marshes," he said. "Where do you belong?"

"I think, I belong there too; I suppose you're throwing for Elke Volkerts!"

"Go!" shouted Hauke and stood in position again. But Ole pushed his head still nearer to him. Then suddenly, before Hauke could do anything against it himself, a hand clutched the intruder and pulled him back, so that the fellow reeled against his comrades. It was not a large hand that had done it; for when Hauke turned his head round for a moment he saw Elke Volkerts putting her sleeve to rights, and her dark brows looked angry in her heated face.

Now something like steely strength shot into Hauke's arm; he bent forward a little, rocked the ball a few times in his hand; then he made the throw, and there was dead silence on both sides. All eyes followed the flying ball, one could hear it whizz as it cut the air; suddenly, already far from the starting point, it was covered by the wings of a silver gull that came flying from the dike with a scream. At the same time, however, one could hear something bang from a distance against the barrel.

"Hurrah for Hauke!" called the people from the marshes, and cries went through the crowd: "Hauke! Hauke Haien has won the game!"

He, however, when all were crowding round him, had thrust his hand to one side to seize another; and even when they called again: "Why are you still standing there, Hauke? The ball is in the barrel!"—he only nodded and did not budge from his place. Only when he felt that the little hand lay fast in his, he said: "You may be right; I think myself I have won."

Then the whole company streamed back and Elke and Hauke were separated and pushed on by the crowd along the road to the inn which ascended from the hill of the dikemaster to the upper land. At this point both escaped the crowd, and while Elke went up to her room, Hauke stood in front of the stable door on the hill and saw how the dark mass of people was gradually wandering up to the parish tavern where a hall was ready for the dancers. Darkness was slowly spreading over the wide land; it was growing calmer and calmer round about, only in the stable behind him the cattle were stirring; from up on the high land he believed that he could already hear the piping of the clarinets in the tavern. Then round the corner of the house he heard the rustling of a dress, and with small steady steps someone was walking along the path that led through the fens up to the high land. Now he discerned the figure walking along in the twilight, and saw that it was Elke; she, too, was going to the dance at the inn. The blood shot up to his neck; shouldn't he run after her and go with her? But Hauke was no hero with women; pondering over this problem, he remained standing still until she had vanished from his sight in the dark.

Then, when the danger of catching up with her was over, he walked along the same way until he had reached the inn by the church, where the chattering and shouting of the crowds in front of the house and in the hall and the shrill sounds of the violins and clarinets surged round him and bewildered his senses. Unobserved he made his way into the Guildhall; but it was not large and so crowded that he could not look a step ahead of him. Silently he stood by the doorpost and looked into the restless swarm. These people seemed to him like fools; he did not have to worry that anyone was still thinking of the match of this afternoon and about who had won the game only an hour ago; everybody thought only of his girl and spun round with her in a circle. His eyes sought only the one, and at last—there! She was dancing with her cousin, the young dike overseer; but soon he saw her no longer, only other girls from the marshes or the high land who did not concern him. Then suddenly the violins and clarinets broke off, and the dance was over; but immediately another one began. An idea shot through Hauke's head—he wondered if Elke would keep her word and if she would not dance by him with Ole Peters. He had almost uttered a scream at this thought; then—yes, what should he do then? But she did not seem to be joining in this dance, and at last it was over. Another one followed, however, a two-step which had just come into vogue here. The music started up madly, the young fellows rushed to their girls, the lights flickered along the walls. Hauke strained his neck to recognise the dancers; and there in the third couple, was Ole Peters—but who was his partner? A broad fellow from the marshes stood in front of her and covered her face! But the dance was raging on, and Ole and his partner were turning out of the crowd. "Vollina! Vollina Harders!" cried Hauke almost aloud, and drew a sigh of relief. But where was Elke? Did she have no partner or had she rejected all because she did not want to dance with Ole? And the music broke off again, and a new dance began; but she was not in sight! There came Ole, still with fat Vollina in his arms! "Well, well," said Hauke; "Jess Harders with his twenty-five acres will soon have to retire too! But where is Elke?"

He left the doorpost and crowded farther into the hall; suddenly he was standing in front of her, as she sat with an older girl friend in a corner. "Hauke!" she called, looking up to him with her narrow face; "are you here? I didn't see you dance."

"I didn't dance," he replied.

"Why not, Hauke?" and half rising she added: "Do you want to dance with me? I didn't let Ole Peters do it; he won't come again!"

But Hauke made no move in this direction: "Thank you, Elke," he said; "I don't know how to dance well enough; they might laugh at you; and then—" he stopped short and looked at her with his whole heart in his grey eyes, as if he had to leave it to them to say the rest.

"What do you mean, Hauke?" she said in a low voice.

"I mean, Elke, the day can't turn out any better for me than it has done already."

"Yes," she said, "you have won the game."

"Elke!" he reproached her almost inaudibly.

Then her face flushed crimson: "Go!" she said; "what do you want?" and she cast down her eyes.

ıen Elke's friend was being drawn away to the dance by a young
ke said louder: "I thought Elke, I had won something better!"

seconds longer her eyes searched the floor; then she raised them
slowly, and a glance met his so full of the quiet power of her nature that it
streamed through him like summer air. "Do as your heart tells you to,
Hauke!" she said; "we ought to know each other!"

Elke did not dance any more that evening, and then, when both went
home, they walked hand in hand. Stars were gleaming in the sky above the
silent marshes; a light east wind was blowing and bringing severe cold with
it; but the two walked on, without many shawls or coverings, as if it had
suddenly turned spring.

Hauke had set his mind on something the fit use for which lay in the
uncertain future; but he had thought of celebrating with it quietly by himself.
So the next Sunday he went into the city to the old goldsmith Andersen and
ordered a strong gold ring. "Stretch out your finger for me to measure! said
the old man and seized his ring-finger. "Well," he said; "yours isn't quite so
big as they usually are with you people!" But Hauke said: "You had better
measure the little finger," and held that one toward him.

The goldsmith looked at him puzzled; but what did he care about the
notions of the young peasant fellows. "I guess we can find one among the
girls' rings" he said, and the blood shot into both of Hauke's cheeks. But the
little gold ring fitted his little finger, and he took it hastily and paid for it with
shining silver; then he put it into his waistcoat pocket while his heart beat
loudly as if he were performing a ceremony. There he kept it thenceforth
every day with restlessness and yet with pride, as if the waistcoat pocket had
no other purpose than to carry a ring.

Thus he carried it for over a year—indeed, the ring even had to wander
into a new waistcoat pocket; the occasion for its liberation had not yet
presented itself. To be sure, it had occurred to him that he might go straight
to his master; his own father was, after all, a landholder too. But when he
was calmer, he knew very well that the old dikemaster would have laughed
at his second man. And so he and the dikemaster's daughter lived on side by
side—she, too, in maidenly silence, and yet both as if they were walking
hand in hand.

A year after that winter holiday Ole Peters had left his position and
married Vollina Harders. Hauke had been right: the old man had retired, and
instead of his fat daughter his brisk son-in-law was riding the brown mare
over the fens and, as people said, on his way back always up the dike. Hauke
was head man now, and a younger one in his place. To be sure, the
dikemaster at first did not want to let him move up. "It's better he stays what

he is," he had growled; "I need him here with my books." But Elke had told him: "Then Hauke will go too, father." So the old man had been scared, and Hauke had been made head man, although he had nevertheless kept on helping the dikemaster with his administration.

But after another year he began to talk with Elke about how his own father's health was failing and told her that the few days in summer that his master allowed him to help on his father's farm were not enough; the old man was having a hard time, and he could not see that any more. It was on a summer evening; both stood in the twilight under the great ash tree in front of the house door. For a while the girl looked up silently into the boughs of the tree; then she replied: "I didn't want to say it, Hauke; I thought you would find the right thing to do for yourself."

"Then I will have to leave your house," he said, "and can't come again."

They were silent for a while and looked at the sunset light which vanished behind the dike in the sea.

"You must know," she said; "only this morning I went to see your father and found him asleep in his armchair; his drawing pen was in his hand and the drawing board with a half-finished drawing lay before him on the table. And when he had waked up and talked to me with effort for a quarter of an hour, and I wanted to go, then he held me back by the hand so full of fear, as if he were afraid it was for the last time; but—"

"But what, Elke?" asked Hauke, when she hesitated to go on.

A few tears ran down the girl's cheeks. "I was only thinking of my father," she said; "believe me, it will be hard for him to get on without you." And then added, as if she had to summon her strength for these words: "It often seems to me as if he too were getting ready for death."

Hauke said nothing; it seemed to him suddenly, as if the ring were stirring in his pocket. But even before he had suppressed his indignation over this involuntary impulse, Elke went on: "No, don't be angry, Hauke; I trust you won't leave us anyway."

Then he eagerly took her hand, and she did not draw it away. For a while the young people stood together in the falling darkness, until their hands slipped apart and each went his way. A gust of wind started and rustled through the leaves of the ash tree and made the shutters rattle on the front of the house; but gradually the night sank down, and quiet lay over the gigantic plain.

Through Elke's persuasion, the old dikemaster had relieved Hauke of his services, although he had not given notice at the right time, and two new hired men were in the house. A few months later Tede Haien died; but before he died, he called his son to his bedside: "Sit by me, my child;" said the old man with his faint voice, "close by me! You don't need to be afraid; he who is near me now is only the dark angel of the Lord who comes to call me."

And his son, deeply affected, sat down close by the dark bed fixed to the wall: "Tell me, father, what you still have to say."

"Yes, my son, there is still something," said the old man and stretched out his hands across the quilt. "When, as a half-grown boy, you went to serve the dikemaster, then you had the idea in your head that you wanted to be one yourself some day. That idea I caught from you, and gradually I came to think that you were the right man for it. But your inheritance was too small for such an office. I have lived frugally during your time of service—I planned to increase it,"

Passionately Hauke seized his father's hands, and the old man tried to sit up, so that he could see him. "Yes, yes, my son," he said; "there in the uppermost drawer of the chest is a document. You know old Antje Wohlers has a fen of five and a half acres; but she could not get on with the rent alone in her crippled old age; so I have always round Martinmas given the poor soul a certain sum, or more when I could; and for that she gave her fen over to me; it is all legally settled. Now she too is on her deathbed; the disease of our marshes, cancer, has seized her; you won't have to pay her any more."

For a while he closed his eyes; then he spoke once more: "It isn't much; but you'll have more then than you were accustomed to with me. May it serve you well in your life on earth!"

With his son's words of thanks in his ears, the old man fell asleep. He had no more cares: and after a few days the dark angel of the Lord had closed his eyes forever, and Hauke received his inheritance.

The day after the funeral Elke came into his house. "Thanks for looking in, Elke," Hauke greeted her.

But she replied: "I'm not looking in; I want to put things in order a little, so that you can live decently in your house. Your father with all his figures and drawings didn't look round much, and the death too makes confusion. I want to make things a little livable for you."

His grey eyes looked full of confidence upon her. "All right, put things in order!" he said; "I like it better that way too."

And then she began to clear up: the drawing board, which was still lying there, was dusted and carried up to the attic, drawing pens and pencil and chalk were locked away carefully in a drawer of the chest; then the young servant girl was called in to help and the furniture was put into different and better positions in the room, so that it seemed as if it now had grown lighter and bigger. Smiling, Elke said: "Only we women can do that," and Hauke in spite of his mourning for his father, had watched her with happy eyes, and, where there was need for it, had helped too.

And when toward dusk—it was in the beginning of September—everything was just as she wanted it for him, she took his hand and nodded to him with her dark eyes: "Now come and have supper with us; for I had to promise my father to bring you; then when you go home, you can enter your house in peace."

Then when they came into the spacious living-room of the dikemaster, where the shutters were already closed and the two candles burning on the table, the latter wanted to rise from his armchair, but his heavy body sank back and he only called to his former man: "That's right, that's right, Hauke, that you've come to see your old friends. Come nearer, still nearer." And when Hauke had stepped up to his chair, he took his hand into both of his own: "Now, now, my boy," he said, "be calm now, for we all must die, and your father was none of the worst. But Elke, now see that the roast gets on to the table; we have to get strength. There's a great deal of work for us, Hauke! The fall inspection is coming; there's a pile of dike and sluice bills as high as the house; the damage to the dike of the western enclosure the other day—I don't know where my head is, but yours, thank God, is a good bit younger; you're a good boy, Hauke."

And after this long speech, with which the old man had laid bare his whole heart, he let himself drop back into his chair and blinked longingly toward the door, through which Elke was just coming in with the roast on the platter. Hauke stood smiling beside him. "Now sit down," said the dikemaster, "so that we won't lose time for nothing; that doesn't taste well cold."

And Hauke sat down; it seemed to be taken for granted that he should help to do the work of Elke's father. And when the fall inspection had come and a few more months of the year were gone, he had indeed done the greatest part of the work.

The story-teller stopped and looked round. The scream of a gull had knocked against the window, and out in the hall one could hear a stamping of feet, as if someone were taking the clay off his heavy boots.

The dikemaster and the overseers turned their heads toward the door of the room. "What is it?" called the first.

A strong man with a southwester on his head had stepped in.

"Sir," he said, "we both have seen it—Hans Nickels and I: the rider on the white horse has thrown himself into the breach."

"Where did you see that?" asked the dikemaster.

"There is only the one break; in Jansen's fen, where the Hauke-Haienland begins."

"Did you see it only once?"

"Only once; it was only like a shadow, but that doesn't mean that this was the first time it happened."

The dikemaster had risen. "You must excuse me," he said, turning to me, "we have to go out and see what this calamity is leading to." Then he left the room with the messenger; the rest of the company too rose and followed him.

I stayed alone with the schoolmaster in the large deserted room; through the curtainless windows, which were now no longer covered by the backs of the guests sitting in front of them, one could have a free view and see how the wind was chasing the dark clouds across the sky.

The old man remained on his seat, with a superior, almost pitying smile on his lips. "It is too empty here now," he said; "may I invite you to my room? I live in this house; and believe me, I know every kind of weather here by the dike—there is nothing for us to fear."

This invitation I accepted with thanks, for I too began to feel chilly, and so we took a light and climbed up the stairs to a room under the gables; there the windows also looked toward the west, but they were covered by woollen rugs. In a bookcase I saw a small library, beside it portraits of two old professors; before a table stood a great high armchair. "Make yourself comfortable," said my pleasant host and threw some pieces of peat into the still faintly glowing stove, which was crowned by a tin kettle on top. "Only wait a little while! The fire will soon roar; then I'll mix you a little glass of grog—that'll keep you awake!"

"I don't need that," I said; "I won't grow sleepy, when I accompany your Hauke upon his life-journey!"

"Do you think so?" and he nodded toward me with his keen eyes, after I had been comfortably settled in his armchair.

Well, where did we leave off? Yes, yes; I know. Well, Hauke had received his inheritance, and as old Antje Wohlers, too, had died of her ailment, his property was increased by her fen. But since the death, or rather, since the last words of his father, something had sprung up within him, the seed of which he had carried in his heart since his boy-hood; he repeated to himself more often than enough that he was the right man for the post if there had to be a new dikemaster. That was it; his father, who had to know, who was the cleverest man in the village, had added his word, like a last gift to his heritage. The fen of the Wohlers woman, for which he had to thank his father too, should be the first stepping-stone to this height. For, to be sure, even with this—a dikemaster had to be able to show more real estate! But his father had got on frugally through his lonely years; and with what he had saved he had made himself owner of new property. This Hauke could do too, and even more; for his father's strength had already been spent, but he could do the hardest work for years. To be sure, even if he should succeed along this line—on account of the sharp methods he had brought into the administration of his old employer, he had made no friends in the village, and Ole Peters, his old antagonist, had just inherited property and was beginning to be a well-to-do man. A row of faces passed before his inner vision, and they all looked at him with hostile eyes. Then a rage against these people seized him: he stretched out his arms as if he would clutch them, for they wanted to push him from the office for which he alone, of all, was destined. These thoughts did not leave him; they were always there again, and so in his young heart there grew beside honor and love, also ambition and hate. But these two he locked up deep within him; even Elke surmised nothing of them.

When the new year had come, there was a wedding; the bride was a relative of the Haiens, and Hauke and Elke were both invited. Indeed, at the wedding dinner it happened that, because a nearer relative was absent, they found themselves seated side by side. Their joy about this was betrayed only by a smile that flitted over the face of each. But Elke to-day sat with indifference in the midst of the noise of chattering and the click of the glasses.

"Is something ailing you?" asked Hauke.

"Oh, really nothing; only there are too many people here for me."

"But you look so sad!"

She shook her head; then again she said nothing.

Then something like jealousy rose within him on account of her silence, and secretly, under the overhanging table-cloth, he seized her hand. She did not draw it away, but clasped it, as if full of confidence, round his. Had a feeling of loneliness come over her, as she had to watch the failing body of her father every day? Hauke did not think of asking her this; but his breathing stopped, as he pulled the gold ring from his pocket. "Will you let it stay?" he asked trembling, while he pushed the ring on the ring-finger of the slender hand.

Opposite them at the table sat the pastor's wife; she suddenly laid down her fork and turned to her neighbor: "My faith, look at that girl!" she cried; "she is turning deadly pale!"

But the blood was returning into Elke's face. "Can you wait, Hauke?" she asked in a low voice.

Clever Frisian though he was, he nevertheless had to stop and think a few seconds. "For what?" he asked then.

"You know perfectly well; I don't need to tell you."

"You are right," he said; "yes, Elke, I can wait—if it's within a human limit."

"Oh, God, I'm afraid, a very near one! Don't talk like that, Hauke; you are speaking of my father's death!" She laid her other hand on her breast; "Till then," she said, "I shall wear the gold ring here; you shan't be afraid of getting it back in my lifetime!"

Then both smiled, and their hands pressed each other so tightly that on other occasions the girl would have cried out aloud.

The pastor's wife meanwhile had looked incessantly at Elke's eyes, which were now glowing like dark fire under the lace fringe of her little gold brocade cap. But in the growing noise at the table she had not understood a word; neither did she turn to her partner again, for she was accustomed not to disturb budding marriages—and this seemed to be such a case—if only for the sake of the promise of the wedding-fee for her husband, who did the marrying.

Elke's presentiment had come true; one morning after Easter the dikemaster Tede Volkerts had been found dead in his bed. When one looked at his face, one could see written upon it that his end had been calm. In the last months he had often expressed a weariness of life; his favorite roast, even his ducks, wouldn't please him any more.

And now there was a great funeral in the village. Up on the high land in the burying-ground round the church there was on the western side a burial-place surrounded by a wrought-iron fence. Upright against a weeping willow stood a broad blue tombstone upon which was hewn the image of death with many teeth in the skeleton jaws; beneath it one could read in large letters:

"Ah, death all earthly things devours,
Takes art and knowledge that was ours;
The mortal man at rest here lies—
God give, that blessèd he may rise."

It was the burial-place of the former dikemaster Volkert Tedsen; now a new grave had been dug in which his son, Tede Volkerts, was to be buried. And now the funeral procession was coming up from the marshes, a multitude of carriages from all parish villages. Upon the first one stood the heavy coffin, and the two shining black horses of the dikemaster's stable drew it up the sandy hill to the high land; their tails and manes were waving in the sharp spring breeze. The graveyard round the church was filled with people up to the ramparts; even on the walled gate boys were perching with little children in their arms; all wanted to see the burying.

In the house down in the marshes Elke had prepared the funeral meal in the best parlour and the living-room. Old wine was set on the table in front of the plates; by the plate of the dikemaster general—for he, too, was not missing to-day—and of the pastor there was a bottle of "Langkork" for each. When everything was ready, she went through the stable in front of the yard door; she met no one on the way, for the hired men were at the funeral with two carriages. Here she stood still and while her mourning clothes were waving in the spring wind, she watched the last carriages down in the village drive up to the church. There after a while a great turmoil appeared, which seemed to be followed by a deadly silence. Elke folded her hands; now they must be letting the coffin into the grave: "And to dust thou shalt return!" Inevitably, in a low voice, as if she could have heard them from up here, she repeated the words. Then her eyes filled with tears, her hands folded across her breast sank into her lap. "Our Father, who art in heaven!" she prayed ardently. And when the Lord's prayer was finished, she stood a long time motionless—she, now the mistress of this great marsh farm; and thoughts of death and of life began to struggle within her.

A distant rumbling waked her. When she opened her eyes, she again saw one carriage after another drive rapidly down from the marshes and up to her farm. She straightened herself, looked ahead sharply once more and then went back, as she had come, through the stable into the solemnly ordered living-rooms. Here too there was nobody; only through the wall could she hear the bustle of the maids in the kitchen. The festive board looked so quiet and deserted; the mirror between the windows had been covered with white scarfs, and likewise the brass knobs of the stove; there was nothing bright any more in the room. Elke saw that the doors of the alcove-bed, in which her father had slept his last sleep were open and she went up and closed them fast. Almost absently she read the proverb that was written on them in golden letters between roses and carnations:

"If thou thy day's work dost aright,
Then sleep comes by itself at night."

That was from her grandfather! She cast a glance at the sideboard; it was almost empty. But through the glass doors she could still see the cut-glass goblet which her father, as he used to tell with relish, had once won as a prize when riding the ring in his youth. She took it out and set it in front of the dikemaster general's plate. Then she went to the window, for already she heard the carriages drive up the hill; one after the other they stopped in front of her house, and, more briskly than they had come, the guests leaped from their seats to the ground. Rubbing their hands and chattering, all crowded into the room; it was not long before they sat down at the festive board, where the well-prepared dishes were steaming—in the best parlor the dikemaster general and the pastor. And noise and loud talking ran along the table, as if death had never spread its awful stillness here. Silent, with her eyes upon her guests, Elke walked round the tables with her maids, to see that nothing was missing at the funeral meal. Hauke Haien, too, sat in the living-room with Ole Peters and other small landowners.

When the meal was over, the white pipes were taken out of the corner and lighted, and Elke was again busy offering the filled coffee cups to her guests; for there was no economy in coffee, either, on this day. In the living-room, at the desk of the man just buried, the dikemaster general stood talking with the pastor and the white-haired dike overseer Jewe Manners.

"Well, gentlemen," said the former; "we have buried the old dikemaster with honor; but where shall we get the new one? I think, Manners, you will have to make up your mind to accept this dignity."

Old Manners smiled and lifted his little black velvet cap from his white hair: "Mr. Dikemaster General," he said, "the game would be too short then; when the deceased Tede Volkers was made dikemaster I was made overseer and have been now for forty years."

"That is no defect, Manners; then you know the affairs all the better and won't have any trouble with them."

But the old man shook his head: "No, no, your Honor, leave me where I am, then I can run along with the rest for a few years longer."

The pastor agreed with him: "Why not give the office," he said, "to the man who has actually managed the affairs in the last years?"

The dikemaster general looked at him: "I don't understand you, pastor!"

But the pastor pointed with his finger to the best parlor, where Hauke in a slow serious manner seemed to be explaining something to two older people. "There he stands," he said; "the long Frisian over there with the keen grey eyes, the bony nose and the high, projecting forehead. He was the old man's hired man and now has his own little place; to be sure, he is rather young."

"He seems to be about thirty," said the dikemaster general, inspecting the man thus presented to him.

"He is scarcely twenty-four," remarked the overseer Manners; "but the pastor is right: all the good work that has been done with dikes and sluices and the like in the last years through the office of dikemaster has been due to him; the old man couldn't do much toward the end."

"Indeed?" said the dikemaster general; "and you think, he would be the right man to move up into the office of his old master?"

"He would be absolutely the right man," replied Jewe Manners; "but he lacks what they call here 'clay under one's feet;' his father had about fifteen, he may well have twenty acres; but with that nobody has yet been made dikemaster."

The pastor had already opened his mouth, as if he wanted to object, when Elke Volkers, who had been in the room for a while, spoke to them suddenly: "Will your Honor allow me a word?" she said to the dikemaster general; "I am speaking only to prevent a mistake from turning into a wrong."

"Then speak, Miss Elke," he replied; "wisdom always sounds well from the lips of pretty girls."

"It isn't wisdom, your Honor; I only want to tell the truth."

"That too one must be able to hear, Miss Elke."

The girl let her dark eyes glance sideways, as if she wanted to make sure that there were no superfluous ears about: "Your Honor," she began then, and her breast heaved with a stronger motion, "my godfather, Jewe Manners, told you that Hauke Haien owned only about twenty acres; that is quite true in this moment, but as soon as it will be necessary, Hauke will call his own just so many more acres as my father's, now my own farm, contains. All that together ought to be enough for a dikemaster."

Old Manners stretched his white head toward her, as if he had to see who was talking there: "What is that?" he said; "child, what are you talking about?"

But Elke pulled a gleaming gold ring on a black ribbon out of her bodice: "I am engaged, godfather Manners," she said; "here is my ring, and Hauke Haien is my betrothed."

"And when—I think I may ask that, as I held you at your baptism, Elke Volkerts—when did that happen?"

"That happened some time ago; but I was of age, godfather Manners," she said; "my father's health had already fallen off, and as I knew him, I thought I had better not get him excited over this; now that he is with God, he will see that his child is in safekeeping with this man. I should have kept still about it through the year of mourning; but for the sake of Hauke and of the diked-in land, I had to speak." And turning to the dikemaster general, she added: "Your Honor will please forgive me."

The three men looked at one another; the pastor laughed, the old overseer limited himself to a "hm, hm!" while the dikemaster general rubbed his forehead as if he were about to make an important decision. "Yes, dear miss," he said at last, "but how about marriage property rights here in this district? I must confess I am not very well versed in these things at this moment in all this confusion."

"You don't need to be, your Honor," replied the daughter of the dikemaster, "before my wedding I shall make my goods over to my betrothed. I have my little pride too," she added smiling; "I want to marry the richest man in the village."

"Well, Manners," said the pastor, "I think you, as godfather, won't mind if I join the young dikemaster with the old one's daughter!"

The old man shook his head gently: "Our Lord give His blessing!" he said devoutly.

But the dikemaster general gave the girl his hand: "You have spoken truly and wisely, Elke Volkerts; I thank you for your firm explanations and hope to be a guest in your house in the future, too, on happier occasions than today. But that a dikemaster should have been made by such a young lady—that is the wonderful part of this story!"

"Your Honor," replied Elke and looked at the kindly high official with her serious eyes, "a true man ought to be allowed the help of his wife!" Then she went into the adjoining parlor and laid her hand silently in that of Hauke Haien.

Several years had gone by: in the little house of Tede Haien now lived a vigorous workman with his wife and child; the young dikemaster Hauke Haien lived with his wife Elke Volkerts on the farm of her father. In summer the mighty ash tree murmured as before in front of the house; but on the bench that now stood beneath it, the young wife was usually seen alone in the evening, sitting with some sewing in her hands; there was no child yet from this marriage. The husband had other things to do than to sit in front of his house door, for, in spite of his having helped in the old man's management before, there was still a multitude of labors to be done which, in those other times, he had not found it wise to touch upon; but now everything had to be cleared up gradually, and he swept with a stiff broom. Besides that, there was the management of the farm, enlarged by his own land, especially as he was trying to save a second hired man. So it came about that, except on Sundays, when they went to church, the two married people saw each other usually only during dinner, which Hauke ate with great haste, and at the rise and close of day; it was a life of continuous work, although one of content.

Then a troublesome rumor started. When one Sunday, after church, a somewhat noisy company of young land-owners from the marshes and the higher land had stayed over their cups at the inn, they talked, when it came to the fourth and fifth glass, not about the king and the government, to be sure—they did not soar so high in those days—but about communal and higher officials, specially about the taxes demanded of the community. And the longer they talked, the less there was that found mercy in their eyes, particularly not the new dike taxes. All the sluices and locks had always held out before, and now they have to be repaired; always new places were found on the dike that required hundreds of cartloads of earth—the devil take the whole affair!

"That's all on account of your clever dikemaster," cried one of the people of the higher land, "who always goes round pondering and sticks his finger into every pie!"

"Yes, he is tricky and wants to win the favor of the dikemaster general; but we have caught him!"

"Why did you let him be thrust on you?" said the other; "now you have to pay in cash."

Ole Peters laughed. "Yes, Marten Fedders, that's the way it is here, and it can't be helped: the old one was made dikemaster on account of his father, the new one on account of his wife." The laughter which ran round the table showed how this sally was appreciated.

But as it had been spoken at the public table of an inn, it did not stay there, and it was circulated in the village of the high land as well as that of the marshes below; and so it reached Hauke. Again the row of ill-meaning faces passed by his inner eye, and he heard the laughter round the tavern table more jeering than it really was. "Dogs!" he shouted, and his eyes looked grimly to the side, as if he wanted to have these people whipped.

Then Elke laid her hand upon his arm: "Let them be; they all would like to be what you are."

"That's just it," he replied angrily.

"And," she went on, "didn't Ole Peters better himself by marriage?"

"He did, Elke; but what he married with Vollina wasn't enough to be dikemaster on."

"Say rather: he wasn't enough," and Elke turned her husband round so that he had to look into the mirror, for they stood between the windows in their room. "There is the dikemaster!" she said; "now look at him; only he who can manage an office has it."

"You're not wrong," he replied pensively, "and yet—Well, Elke, I have to go to the eastern lock; the gates won't close again."

He went; but he was not gone long, before the repairing of the lock was forgotten. Another idea, which he had only half thought out and carried round with him for years, which, however, had been pushed back by the urgent affairs of his office, now took hold of him again and more powerfully than before, as if he had suddenly grown wings.

Before he was really aware of it himself, he found himself on the sea-dike a good way south toward the city; the village that lay on this side had some time ago vanished to the left. He was still walking on, fixing his eyes constantly on the seaward side of the broad foreland. If some one had walked beside him, he must have seen what concentrated mental work was going on behind those eyes. At last he stood still: the foreland here dwindled into a narrow strip along the dike. "It will have to work!" he said to himself. "Seven years in the office—they shan't say any more that I am dikemaster only because of my wife."

He was still standing there, and his eyes swept sharply and thoughtfully on all sides over the green foreland. Then he walked back until, here too, the broad plain that lay before him ended in a narrow strip of green pastureland. Through this, close by the dike, shot a strong arm of the sea which divided almost the whole foreland from the mainland and made it an island; a crude wooden bridge led to it, so that one could go back and forth with cattle or teams of hay or grain. It was low tide now, and the golden September sun was glistening on the strip of wet clay, about a hundred feet broad, and on the deep channel in the middle of it through which the sea was even now driving its waters. "That can be damned!" said Hauke to himself, after he had watched this playing of the water for a while. Then he looked up, and on from the dike upon which he stood, past the channel, he drew an imaginary line along the edge of the isolated land, round toward the south and back again to the east over the eastern continuation of the channel, up to the dike. But the line which he had drawn invisibly was a new dike, new also in the construction of its outline, which as yet existed only in his head.

"That would make dammed-in land of about a thousand acres," he said smiling to himself; "not so large; but—"

Another calculation came into his mind: the foreland here belonged to the community, or rather, a number of shares to the single members, according to the size of their property in the municipality or other legal income. He began to count up how many shares he had received from his father and how many from Elke's father, and how many he had already bought during his marriage, partly with a dim foreboding of future gain, partly because of his increased sheep stock. It was a considerable lot; for he had also bought all of Ole Peter's shares when the latter had been disgusted because his best ram had been drowned, once when the foreland had been partly flooded. What excellent pasture and farm land that must make and how valuable it would be if it were all surrounded by his new dike! Like intoxication this idea rose into his brain; but he pressed his nails into the hollows of his hands and forced his eyes to see clearly and soberly what lay there before him: a great plain without a dike exposed to who knew what storms and floods in the next years, and at its outermost edge a herd of dirty sheep now wandering and grazing slowly. That meant a heap of work, struggle, and annoyance for him! In spite of all that, as he was walking on the footpath down from the dike across the fens toward his hill, he felt as if he were carrying home a great treasure.

In the hall Elke came to meet him: "How about the lock?" she asked.

He looked down at her with a mysterious smile: "We shall soon need another lock," he said; "and sluices and a new dike."

"I don't understand," returned Elke, as they walked into the room; "what do you want to do, Hauke?"

"I want," he began slowly and then stopped for a second, "I want the big foreland that begins opposite our place and stretches on westward to be diked in and made into a solid enclosure. The high floods have left us in peace for almost a generation now; but when one of the bad ones comes again and destroys the growth down there—then all at once there'll be an end to all this glory. Only the old slackway has let things stay like this till to-day."

She looked at him with astonishment: "Why, you are scolding yourself!" she said.

"I am, Elke; but till now there were so many other things to do."

"Yes, Hauke; surely, you have done enough."

He had sat down in the armchair of the old dikemaster, and his hands were clutching both arms fast.

"Have you the courage for it?" his wife asked him.

"I have that, Elke," he spoke hastily.

"Don't be too hasty, Hauke; that work is a matter of life and death; and almost all the people will be against you, they won't thank you for your labor and trouble."

He nodded. "I know that!" he said.

"And if it will only succeed," she cried again, "ever since I was a child I heard that the channel can't be stopped up, and that therefore one shouldn't touch it."

"That was an excuse for the lazy ones!" said Hauke; "why shouldn't one be able to stop up the channel?"

"That I have not heard; perhaps because it goes right through; the rush of the water is too strong." A remembrance came over her and an almost mischievous smile gleamed out of her serious eyes: "When I was a child," she told, "I heard our hired men talk about it once; they said, if a dam was to hold there, some live thing would have to be thrown into the hold and diked up with the rest; when they were building a dike on the other side, about a hundred years ago, a gipsy child was dammed in that they had bought from its mother for a lot of money. But now I suppose no one would sell her child."

Hauke shook his head: "Then it is just as well that we have none; else they would do nothing less than demand it of us."

"They shouldn't get it!" said Elke and folded her arms across her body as if in fear.

And Hauke smiled; but she asked again: "And the huge cost? Have you thought of that?"

"I have, Elke; what we will get out of it will far surpass the cost; even the cost of keeping up the old dike will be covered a good bit by the new one. We do our own work and there are over eight teams of horses in the community, and there is no lack of young strong arms. At least you shan't have made me dikemaster for nothing, Elke; I want to show them that I am one!"

She had been crouching in front of him and looking at him full of care; now she rose with a sigh. "I have to go back to my day's work," she said, and gently stroked his cheek; "you do yours, Hauke."

"Amen, Elke!" he said with a serious smile; "there is work enough for us both."

There was truly work enough for both, but the heaviest burden was now on the man's shoulder. On Sunday afternoons, often too in the evenings, Hauke sat together with a good surveyor, deep in calculations, drawings and plans; when he was alone, he did the same and often did not stop till long after midnight. Then he would slip into their common sleeping-room—for the stuffy beds fixed to the wall in the living-room were no longer used in Hauke's household—and his wife would lie with her eyes closed, pretending to sleep, so that he would get his rest at last, although she was really waiting for him with a beating heart. Then he would sometimes kiss her forehead and say a low word of love, and then lie down to sleep, though sleep often did not come to him before the first crowing of the cock. In the winter storms he ran out on the dike with pencil and paper in his hand, and stood and made drawings and took notes while a gust of wind would tear his cap from his head and make his long, light hair fly round his heated face. Soon, as long as the ice did not bar his way, he rowed with a servant out into the sea and with plumb line and rods measured the depths of the currents about which he was not yet sure. Often enough Elke trembled for his life, but when he was safely back, he could hardly have noticed anything, except by the tight clasp of her hand or by the bright lightning that gleamed from her usually so quiet eyes. "Have patience, Elke," he said once when it seemed to him as if his wife would not let him alone; "I have to have the whole thing clear to myself

The Rider on the White Horse

before I propose it." Then she nodded and let him be. There were no le͟s͟ rides into the city, either, to see the dikemaster general, and all these and the labors for house and farm were always followed by work late into the night. His intercourse with other people outside of his work and business vanished almost entirely; even with his wife it grew less and less. "These are bad times, and they will last long yet," said Elke to herself and went to her work.

At last, when sun and spring winds had broken the ice everywhere, the last work in preparation had been done. The petition to the dikemaster general, to be seconded by a higher official, contained the proposal that the foreland should be diked for the promoting of the general weal, particularly of the diked-in district, as well as the ruler's treasury, as this would receive in a few years the taxes from about a thousand acres. This was neatly copied and put into a firm envelope together with the corresponding drafts and plans of all the positions, present and future, of the locks and sluices and everything else that belonged to the project; and this was sealed with the official seal of the dikemaster.

"Here it is, Elke," said the young dikemaster; "now give it your blessing."

Elke laid her hand into his: "We want to stand by each other," she said.

"Yes, we do."

Then the petition was sent into the city by a messenger on horseback.

I must call your attention to the fact, dear sir, the school-master interrupted his account, fixing his eyes pleasantly upon me, that what I have told you up to this point I have gathered during my activity of almost forty years in this district from the traditions of intelligent people or from the tales of their grandchildren and great-grandchildren. What I am about to tell you now, so that you may find the right connection between what has gone before and the final outcome of my story, used to be and is still the talk of the whole marsh village, as soon as the spinning-wheels begin to whir round All Saints' Day.

If one stood on the dike, about five or six hundred feet to the north of the dikemaster's farm, one could, at that time, look a few thousand feet out over the sea, and somewhat farther from the opposite shore one could see a little island, which they called "Jeverssand," or "Jevers Island." Our forefathers of that generation had used it as a pasture for sheep, for at that time grass was still growing on it; but even that had stopped, because the low island had several times been flooded by the sea, and in midsummer too, so that the growth of grass was stunted and made useless as a sheep pasture. So it happened that the island had no more visitors except gulls and other birds and occasionally a sea eagle; and on moonlight nights from the dike one could only see the light or heavy mists pass over it. And people believed that, when the moon shone upon the island from the east, they could recognise a few bleached skeletons of drowned sheep and that of a horse, although, to be sure, no one could understand how it had come there.

It was at the end of March that the day laborer from the house of Tede Haien and Iven Johns, the hired man of the young dikemaster, stood beside each other at that place and without stirring stared at the island which could scarcely be recognised in the dim moonshine; but something out of the ordinary seemed to hold them there. The laborer put his hands into his pockets and shuddered: "Come, Iven," he said; "there's nothing good in that; let us go home."

The other laughed, even though horror sounded through his laughter: "Oh, bosh, it's a live creature, a big one! Who the devil has chased it on to the clay out there? Look, now it's stretching its neck our way! No, it's drooping its head; it is feeding. I'd have thought, there was nothing to feed on there! What can it be?"

"That's not our business!" replied the other. "Good night, Iven, if you don't want to go with me; I'm going home!"

"Oh, yes; you've got a wife, you can go into your warm bed! But I've got a lot of March air in my room!"

"Good night, then," the laborer called back, as he marched home on the dike. The hired man looked round a few times after his fleeing companion; but the desire to see something gruesome held him fast. Then a dark, stocky figure came toward him on the dike from the village; it was the servant boy of the dikemaster. "What do you want, Carsten?" the hired man called to him.

"I?—nothing," said the boy; but our master wants to speak to you, Iven Johns."

The man's eyes were drawn back to the island again. "All right, I'm coming right off," he said.

"What are you looking at so?" asked the boy.

The man raised his arm and pointed silently to the island. "Oh, look!" whispered the boy; "there goes a horse—a white horse—the devil must be riding that—how can a horse get to Jevers Island?"

"Don't know, Carsten; if it's only a real horse!"

"Yes, yes, Iven; look, now it's feeding just like a horse! But who has brought it there—we have no boats in the village big enough! Perhaps it's only a sheep; Peter Ohm says by moonlight ten circles of peat look like a whole village. No, look! Now it's jumping around—it must be a horse after all!"

The Rider on the White Horse

Both stood silent for a while, their eyes fixed on what they saw indistinctly going on upon yonder island. The moon stood high in the heavens and shone upon the wide sea what was just beginning, as the tide rose, to wash with its waters over the glistening flats of clay. Only the low murmur of the water, not the sound of a single animal was heard here in the vast open; on the marshes behind the dike, too, all was deserted, and cows and oxen were still in their stalls. Nothing stirred; only the thing that they took for a horse—a white horse—seemed to be moving on Jevers Island. "It is growing lighter," the hired man broke into the silence; "I can see the white sheeps' skeletons shimmer distinctly!"

"I too," said the boy and stretched his neck; but then, as if it came over him suddenly, he pulled the man by the sleeve. "Iven," he gasped, "the horse skeleton, that used to lie there too—where is that? I can't see it!"

"I don't see it either. Strange!" said the man.

"Not so strange, Iven! Sometimes, I don't know in what nights, the bones are supposed to rise and act as if they were alive!"

"Is that so?" said the man; "that's an old wives' story!"

"May be, Iven," said the boy.

"But I thought you were sent to get me. Come, we have to go home. It always stays the same, anyway."

The man could not get the boy away until he had turned him round by force and pushed him on to the way. "Listen, Carsten," said the former, when the ghostly island lay a good way behind him, "you are supposed to be a good sport; I believe you would like to inspect these doings yourself."

"Yes," replied Carsten, still shuddering a little. "Yes, I'd like to do that, Iven."

"Do you really mean that? Then," said the man after he had given his hand to the boy emphatically, "we'll take our boat to-morrow evening; you row to Jeverssand; I'll stay on the dike in the meantime."

"Yes," replied the boy, "that'll work! I'll take my whip with me."

"Do that."

Silently they came near the house of their employers, to which they slowly climbed up the high hill.

At the same hour on the following night the hired man sat on the big stone in front of the stable door, when the boy came to him, snapping his whip. "What a strange sound!" said the former.

"I should say—take care!" returned the boy; "I have stuck nails into the string, too."

"Then come," said the other.

ˈght before, the moon stood in the eastern sky and looked
ɪr light. Soon both were not on the dike again and looked
˲ɪand, that looked like a strip of mist in the water. "There it
_ ˵ again," said the man; "I was here in the afternoon, and then it wasn't
there; but I saw the white horse skeleton lying there distinctly!"

The boy stretched his neck: "That isn't there now, Iven," he whispered.

"Well, Carsten, how is it?" said the man. "Are you still keen on rowing over?"

Carsten stopped to think a moment; then he struck the air with his whip: "Go ahead and slip the mooring, Iven."

But over yonder it seemed as if the creature moving there were stretching its neck and raising its head toward the mainland. They were not seeing it any more; they were already walking down the dike to the place where the boat was moored. "Now get in," said the man, after he had slipped the mooring. "I'll wait till you are back. You'll have to land on the eastern side; that's where one always could land." And the boy nodded silently and rowed away into the moonlit night with his whip; the man wandered back to the foot of the dike and climbed on to it again at the place where they had stood before. Soon he saw how the boat was moored at a steep, dark place, where a broad creek flowed out, and how a stocky figure leaped ashore. Didn't it seem as if the boy were snapping his whip? But then, too, it might be the sound of the rising flood. Several hundred feet to the north he saw what they had taken for a white horse; and how—yes, the figure of the boy came marching straight up to it. Now it raised its head as if it were startled; and the boy—now one could hear it plainly—snapped his whip. But—what was he doing? He was turning round, he was going back the same way he had come. The creature over there seemed to graze on unceasingly; no sound of neighing could be heard; sometimes it seemed as if strips of water were drawn across the apparition. The man gazed as if spellbound.

Then he heard the arrival of the boat at the shore he was on, and soon in the dusk he saw the boy climb toward him up the dike. "Well, Carsten," he asked, "what was it?"

The boy shook his head. "It was nothing!" he said. "From the boat I saw it a short way off; but then, when I was on the island—the devil knows where that animal has hid himself! The moonlight was bright enough; but when I came to that place there was nothing there but the pale bones of a half dozen sheep, and a little farther away lay the horse skeleton, too, with its white, long skull and let the moon shine into its empty sockets."

"Hm!" replied the man; "are you sure you saw right?"

"Yes, Iven, I stood in the place; a forlorn bird that had cowered behind the skeleton for the night flew up screaming so that I was startled and snapped my whip after it a few times."

"And that was all?"

"Yes, Iven; I don't know any more."

"It is enough, too," said the man, then he pulled the boy toward him by the arm and pointed over to the island. "Do you see something over there, Carsten?"

"It's true, there it goes again."

"Again?" said the man; "I've been looking over there all the time, and it hasn't been away at all; you went right up to the monster."

The boy stared at him; all at once horror was in his usually so pert face, and this did not escape the man. "Come," said the latter "let's go home: from here it looks alive and over there is nothing but bones—that's more than you and I can grasp. But keep quiet about it, one mustn't talk of these things."

They turned round and the boy trotted beside him; they did not speak, and by their side the marshes lay in perfect silence.

But when the moon had vanished and the nights were black, something else happened.

At the time when the horse market was going on Hauke Haien had ridden into the city, although he had had nothing to do with the market. Nevertheless, when the came home toward evening, he brought home a second horse. It had rough hair, however, and was lean, so that one could count every rib and its eyes looked tired and sunken deep into the sockets. Elke had stepped out in front of the house door to meet her husband: "Heaven help us!" she cried, "what shall we do with that old white horse?" For when Hauke had ridden up to the house with it and stopped under the ash tree, she had seen that the poor creature was lame, too.

The young dikemaster, however, jumped laughing down from his brown horse: "Never mind, Elke; it didn't cost much, anyway."

The clever woman replied: "You know, the greatest bargain turns out to be the most expensive."

"But not always, Elke; this animal is at most four years old; look at it more carefully. It is starved and has been abused; our oats shall do it good. I'll take care of it myself, so that they won't overfeed it."

Meanwhile the animal stood with bowed head; its long mane hung down its neck. Elke, while her husband was calling the hired men, walked round it with curious eyes; but she shook her head: "A horse like this has never yet been in our stable."

When the servant boy came round the corner, he suddenly stood still with frightened eyes. "Well, Carsten," called the dikemaster, "what has struck you? Don't you like my white horse?"

"Yes—oh, yes, master, why not?"

"Then take the animal into the stable; don't feet it. I'll come myself right off."

The boy took hold of the halter of the white horse carefully and then hastily, as if for protection, seized the bridle of the brown horse also put into his trust. Hauke then went into the room with his wife. She had warm beer ready for him, and bread and butter were there, too.

He had soon finished; then he got up and walked up and down the room with his wife. "Let me tell you, Elke," he said, while the evening glow played on the tiles of the wall, "how I came to get the animal. I spent about an hour at the dikemaster general's; he has good news for me—there will be some departures, here and there, from my drawings; but the main thing, my outline, has been accepted, and the next days may bring the command to begin the new dike."

Elke sighed involuntarily. "After all?" she said, anxiously.

"Yes, wife," returned Hauke; "it will be hard work; but for that, I think, the Lord has brought us together! Our farm is in such good order now, you can take a good part of it on your own shoulders. Think ahead ten years—then we'll own quite a different property."

During his first words she had pressed her husband's hand into hers as a sign of assurance; but his last words could give her no pleasure. "For whom all the property?" she said. "You would have to take another wife then; I shall bring you no children."

Tears shot into her eyes; but he drew her close into his arms. "We'll leave that to the Lord," he said; "but now and at that time too, we are young enough to have joy for ourselves in the fruits of our labors."

She looked at him a long time with her dark eyes while he held her. "Forgive me, Hauke," she said; "sometimes I am a woman in despair."

He bent down to her face and kissed her: "You are my wife and I am your husband, Elke. And nothing can alter that."

Then she clasped her arms tightly round his neck: "You are right, Hauke, and what comes, will come for us both." Then she freed him, blushing. "You wanted to tell me about the white horse," she said in a low voice.

"So I did, Elke, I told you, my head and heart were full of joy over the good news that the dikemaster general had given me. So I was riding back again out of the city, when on the dam, behind the harbor, I met a shabby fellow—I couldn't tell if he was a vagabond, a tinker, or what. This fellow was pulling the white horse after him by the halter; but the animal raised his head and looked at me with dull eyes. It seemed to me as if he wanted to beg me for something—and, indeed, at that moment I was rich enough. 'Hallo, good sir,' I hailed him, 'where do you want to go with your jade?'

"The fellow stopped, and the white horse, too. 'Sell him,' he said, and nodded to me slyly.

"'But spare me!' I called cheerfully.

"'I think I shall!' he said; 'it's a good horse and worth no less than a hundred dollars.'

"I laughed into his face.

"'Well,' he said, 'don't laugh so hard; you don't need to pay it. But I have no use for it, it'll perish with me; with you it would soon look different.'

"Then I jumped down from my brown horse and looked into the white horse's mouth and saw that it was still a young animal. 'How much do you want for it?' I cried, for again the horse seemed to look at me beseechingly.

"'Sir, take it for thirty dollars,' said the fellow, and I'll give you the halter to the bargain.'

"And then, wife, I took the fellow's stretched-out brown hand, which looked almost like a claw. And so we have the white horse, and I think a good enough bargain. The only strange thing was that, when I rode away with the horses, I soon heard laughter behind me, and when I turned round my head, saw the Slovak standing with his legs apart, his arms on his back, and laughing after me like a devil.

"Oh, horror," cried Elke; "I hope that white horse will bring you nothing from his old master. May he thrive for your good, Hauke!"

"Thrive he shall, at least as far as I can make him!" And the dikemaster went into the stable, as he had told the boy a while ago.

But not only on the first night did he feed the white horse—from that time on he always did it himself and did not leave the animal out of sight. He wanted to show that he had mad a first-rate bargain; anyway, he did not want to allow any mistake. And already after a few weeks the animal's condition improved: gradually the rough hair vanished; a smooth, blue-spotted skin appeared, and one day when he led it round on the place, it walked nimbly on its steady legs. Hauke thought of the adventurous seller. "That fellow was a fool, or a knave who had stolen it," he murmured to himself. Then soon, when the horse merely heard his footsteps, it threw back its head and neighed to greet him; and now he saw too that it had, what the Arabs demand of a good horse, a spare face, out of which two fiery brown eyes were gleaming. He would lead it into its stable and put a light saddle on it; and scarcely did he sit on the saddle, when the animal uttered a neigh like a shout of delight.

It sped away with him, down the hill to the road and then to the dike; but the rider sat securely, and when they had reached the top, it went more quietly, easily, as if dancing, and thrust its head to the side of the sea. He patted and stroked its smooth neck, but it no longer needed these endearments, the horse seemed altogether to be one with the rider, and after he had ridden a distance northwards out on the dike, he turned it easily and reached the farm again.

The men stood at the foot of the hill and waited for the return of their master. "Now, John," he cried, as he leaped down from his horse. "you ride it to the fens where the others are; it'll carry you like a cradle."

The white horse shook its head and neighed aloud over the sunny marshes, while the hired man was taking off the saddle and the boy ran with it to the harness-room; then it laid its head on its master's shoulder and suffered him to caress it. But when the hired man wanted to swing himself on its back, it leaped to the side with a sudden bound and then stood motionless, turning its beautiful eyes on its master. "Hallo, Iven," cried Hauke, "has he hurt you?" and he tried to help his man up from the ground.

The latter was busily rubbing his hip: "No, sir, I can manage still; but let the devil ride that white horse!"

"And me!" Hauke added, laughing. "Then bring him to the fens by the bridle."

"And when the man obeyed, somewhat humiliated, the white horse meekly let itself be led.

A few evenings later the man and the boy stood together in front of the stable door. The sunset gleam had vanished behind the dike, the land it enclosed was already wrapped in twilight; only at rare intervals from far off one could hear the lowing of a startled bull or the scream of a lark whose life was ending through the assault of a weasel or a water rat. The man was leaning against the doorpost and smoking his short pipe, from which he could no longer see the smoke; he and the boy had not yet talked together. Something weighed on the boy's soul, however, but he did not know how to begin with the silent man. "Iven," he said finally, "you know that horse skeleton on Jeverssand."

"What about it?" asked the man.

"Yes, Iven, what about it? It isn't there any more—neither by day nor by moonlight; I've run up to the dike about twenty times."

"The old bones have tumbled to pieces, I suppose," said Iven and calmly smoked on.

"But I was out there by moonlight, too; nothing is moving over there on Jeverssand, either!"

The Rider on the White Horse

"Why, yes!" said the man, "if the bones have fallen apart, it won't be a to get up any more."

"Don't joke, Iven! I know now; I can tell you where it is."

The man turned to him suddenly: "Well, where is it, then?"

"Where?" repeated the boy emphatically. "It is standing in our stable; there it has been standing, ever since it was no more on the island. It isn't for nothing that our master always feeds it himself; I know about it, Iven."

For a while the man puffed away violently into the night. "You're not right in your mind, Carsten," he said then; "our white horse? If ever a horse was alive, that one is. How can a wide-awake youngster like you get mixed up with such an old wives' belief!"

But the boy could not be converted: if the devil was inside the white horse, why shouldn't it be alive? On the contrary, it was all the worse. He started, frightened, every time that he stepped into the stable toward night, where the creature was sometimes kept in summer and it turned its fiery head toward him so violently. "The devil take you!" he would mutter; "we won't stay together much longer!"

So he secretly looked round for a new place, gave notice and, about All Saints' Day, went to Ole Peters as hired man. Here he found attentive listeners for his story of the dikemaster's devil's horse. Fat Mrs. Vollina and her dull-witted father, the former dike overseer, Jess Harders, listened in smug horror and afterwards told it to all who had a grudge against the dikemaster in their hearts or who took pleasure in that kind of thing.

In the mean time already at the end of March the order to begin on the new dike had arrived from the dikemaster general. Hauke first called the dike overseers together, and in the inn up by the church they had all appeared one day and listened while he read to them the main points from the documents that had been drawn up so far: points from his petition from the report of the dikemaster general, and lastly the final order in which, above all, the outline which he had proposed was accepted, so that the new dike should not be steep like the old ones, but slant gradually toward the sea. But they did not listen with cheerful or even satisfied faces.

"Well, yes," said an old dike overseer, "here we have the whole business now, and protests won't do any good, because the dikemaster general patronises our dikemaster."

"You're right, Detlev Wiens," added a second; "our spring work is waiting, and now a dike miles long is to be made—then everything will have to be left undone."

"You can finish all that this year," said Hauke; "things don't move as fast as that."

Few wanted to admit that. "But your profile," said a third, bringing up something new; "the dike will be as broad on the outside toward the water as other things are long. Where shall we get the material? When shall the work be done?"

"If not this year, then next year; that will depend chiefly on ourselves," said Hauke.

Angry laughter passed along the whole company. "But what is all that useless labor for? The dike isn't supposed to be any bigger than the old one;" cried a new voice; "and I'm sure that's stood for over thirty years."

"You are right," said Hauke, "thirty years ago the old dike broke; then backwards thirty-five years ago, and again forty-five years ago; but since then, although it is still standing steep and senseless, the highest floods have spared us. But the new dike is to stand in spite of such floods for hundreds of years; for it will not be broken through; because the gentle slope toward the sea gives the waves no point of attack, and so you will gain safe land for yourselves and your children, and that is why the government and the dikemaster general support me—and, besides, that is what you ought to be aware of for your own profit."

When the assembled were not ready on the spot to answer these words, an old white-haired man rose with difficulty from his chair. It was Elke's godfather, Jewe Manners, who, in response to Hauke's beseeching, had kept his office as dike overseer.

"Dikemaster Hauke Haien," he said, "you give us much commotion and expense, and I wish you had waited with all this until the Lord had called me to rest; but—you are right, and only unreason can deny that. We ought to thank God every day that He has kept us our precious piece of foreland against storms and the force of the tide, in spite of our idleness; now, I believe, is the eleventh hour, in which we must lend a hand and try to save it for ourselves to the best of our knowledge and powers, and not defy God's patience any longer. I, my friends, am an old man; I have seen dikes built and broken; but the dike that Hauke Haien has proposed according to his God-given insight and has carried through with the government—that dike none of you living men will see broken. And if you don't want to thank him yourselves, your grandchildren some day will not deny him his laurel wreath."

Jewe Manners sat down again; he took his blue handkerchief from his pocket and wiped a few drops from his forehead. The old man was still known as a man of efficiency and irreproachable integrity, and as the assembly was not inclined to agree with him, it remained silent. But Hauke Haien took the floor, though all saw that he had grown pale.

"I thank you, Jewe Manners," he said, "for staying here and for what you have said. You other gentlemen, have the goodness at least to consider the building of the new dike, which indeed will be my burden, as something that cannot be helped any more, and let us decide accordingly what needs to be done."

"Speak!" said one of the overseers. And Hauke spread the map of the new dike out on the table.

"A while ago someone has asked," he began, "from where we shall get the soil? You see, as far as the foreland stretches out into the flooded district, a strip of land is left free outside of the dike line; from this we can take our soil and from the foreland which runs north and south along the dike from the new enclosed land. If we have a good layer of clay at the water side, at the inside and the middle we can take sand. Now first we have to get a surveyor to mark off the line of the new dike on the foreland. The one who helped me work out my plan will be best suited for the work. Furthermore we have to order some one-horse tip-carts at a cartwright's for the purpose of getting our clay and other material. For damming the channel and also for the inside, where we may have to use sand, we shall need—I cannot tell now how many cartloads of straw for the dike, perhaps more than can be spared in the marshes. Let us discuss then now how all this is to be acquired and arranged. The new lock here, too, on the west side toward the water will have to be given over to an efficient carpenter later for repairs."

The assembly gathered round the table, looked at the map with half attention and gradually began to talk; but it seemed as if they did it merely so that there might be some talking. When it came to the choice of a surveyor, one of the younger ones remarked: "You have thought it out, dikemaster; you must know best yourself who is fit for it."

But Hauke replied: "As you are sworn men, you have to speak your own opinion, Jacob Meyen; and if you think of something better, I'll let my proposal fall."

"Oh, I guess it'll be all right," said Jacob Meyen.

But one of the older ones did not think it would be so perfectly all right. He had a nephew, a surveyor, the like of whom had never been in the marshes, who was said to surpass the dikemaster's father, the late Tede Haien.

So there was a discussion about the two surveyors and it was finally decided to let both do the work together. There was similar disputing over the carts, the furnishing of the straw and everything else, and Hauke came home late and almost exhausted on his brown horse which he was still riding at that time. But when he sat in the old armchair, handed down from his self-important but more easy-going predecessor, his wife was quickly at his side: "You look tired, Hauke, she said, and with her slender hand pushed his hair out of his forehead.

"A little, I suppose," he replied.

"And is it getting on?"

"It'll get on;" he said with a bitter smile; "but I myself have to push the wheels and have to be glad if they aren't kept back."

"But not by all?"

"No, Elke; your godfather, Jewe Manners, is a good man; I wish he were thirty years younger."

When after a few weeks the dike line had been marked off and most of the carts had been furnished, the dikemaster had gathered together in the inn by the church all the shareholders of the land to be diked in and also the owners of the land behind the old dike. He wanted to present to them a plan for the distribution of the work and the cost and to hear their possible objections; for the owners of the old land had to bear their part of the labor land the cost because the new dike and the new sluices would lessen the running expenses of the older ones. This plan had been a hard piece of work for Hauke and if he had not been given a dike messenger and a dike clerk through the mediation of the dikemaster general, he could not have accomplished it so soon, although again he was working well into the night. When he went to bed, tired to death, his wife no longer waited for him with feigned sleep; she, too, had such a full share of daily work that she lay, as if at the bottom of a deep well, in a sleep that could not be disturbed.

Now Hauke read his plan and again spread his papers out on the table—papers which, to be sure, had already lain for three days in the inn for inspection. Some serious men were present, who regarded this conscientious diligence with awe, and who, after quiet consideration, submitted to the low charge of the dikemaster. But others, whose shares in the new land had been sold either by themselves or their fathers or someone else who had bought them, complained because they had to pay part of the expenses of the new diked-in land which no longer concerned them, not thinking that through the new work the old lands would be less costly to keep up. Again there were others who were blessed with shares for the new land who clamoured that one should buy these of them for very little, because they wanted to be rid of shares that burdened them with such unreasonable labor. Old Peters who was leaning against the doorpost with a grim face, shouted into the midst: "Think first and then trust in our dikemaster! He knows how to calculate; he already had most of the shares, then he was clever enough to get mine at a bargain, and when he had them, he decided to dike in the new land."

After these words for a moment a deadly silence fell upon the assembly. The dikemaster stood by the table where he had spread out his papers before; he raised his head and looked over to Old Peters: "You know very well, Ole Peters," he said, "that you are libeling me; you are doing it just the same, because you know that, nevertheless, a good part of the dirt you are throwing at me will cling to me. The truth is that you wanted to be rid of your shares, and that at that time I needed them for my sheep raising. And if you want to know more I will tell you that the dirty words which escaped your lips here at the inn, namely that I was made dikemaster only on account of my wife—that they have stirred me up and I wanted to show you all that I could be dikemaster on my own account. And so, Ole Peters, I have done what the dikemaster before me ought to have done. If you are angry, though, because at that time your shares were made mine—you hear now, there are enough who want to sell theirs cheaply, because the work connected with them is too much."

There was applause from a small part of the assembled men, and old Jewe Manners, who stood among them, cried aloud: "Bravo, Hauke Haien! The Lord will let your work succeed!"

But they did not finish after all, although Ole Peters was silent, and the people did not disperse till supper time. Not until they had a second meeting was everything settled, and then only after Hauke had agreed to furnish four teams in the next month instead of the three that were his share.

At last, when the Whitsuntide bells were ringing through the land, the work had begun: unceasingly the dumpcarts were driven from the foreland to the dike line, there to dump the clay, and in the same way an equal number was driven back to get new clay from the foreland. At the line of the dike itself men stood with shovels and spades in order to put the dumped clay into its right place and to smooth it. Huge loads of straw were driven up and taken down. This straw was not only used to cover the lighter material, like sand and loose earth, which was used for the inside; gradually single pieces of the dike were finished, and the sod with which they were covered was in places securely overlaid with straw as a protection against the gnawing waves. Inspectors engaged for the purpose walked back and forth, and when it was stormy, they stood with wide open mouths and shouted their orders through wind and storm. In and out among them rode the dikemaster on his white horse, which he now used exclusively, and the animal flew back and forth with its rider, while he have his orders quickly and drily, praised the workmen, or, as it happened sometimes, dismissed a lazy or clumsy man without mercy. "That can't be helped!" he would cry; "we can't have the dike spoiled on account of your laziness!" From far, when he came up from the enclosed land below, they heard the snorting of his horse, and all hands went to work more briskly. "Come on, get to work! There's the rider on the white horse!"

During breakfast time, when the workmen sat together in masses on the ground, with their morning bread, Hauke rode along the deserted works, and his eyes were sharp to spy where slovenly hands had used the spade. Then when he rode up to the men and explained to them how the work ought to be done, they would look up at him and keep on chewing their bread patiently; but he never heard a word of assent or even any remark. Once at this time of day, though rather late, when he had found the work on a part of the dike particularly well done, he rode to the nearest assembly of breakfasting men, jumped down from his white horse and asked cheerfully who had done such a neat day's work. But they only looked at him shyly and sombrely and only slowly, as if against their will, a few names were given. The man to whom he had given his horse, which stood as meekly as a lamb, held it with both hands and looked as if he were frightened at the animal's beautiful eyes fixed, as usual, upon its master.

"Well, Marten," Hauke called to him: "why do you stand there as if you had been thunderstruck?"

"Sir, your horse is so calm, as if it were planning something bad!"

Hauke laughed and took the horse by the reins himself, when immediately it rubbed its head caressingly against his shoulder. Some of the workmen looked shyly at horse and rider, others ate their morning meal silently, as if all this were no concern of theirs, and now and then threw a crumb to the gulls who had remembered this feeding place and with their slender wings almost descended on the heads of the men. For a while the dikemaster gazed absently at the begging birds as they chased with their bills the bits thrown at them; then he leaped to his saddle and rode away, without turning round to look at the men. Some of the words that now were being spoken among them sounded to him like derision. "What can that mean?" he spoke to himself. "Was Elke right when she said that all were against me? These laborers and poorer people, too, many of whom will be well off through my new dike?"

He spurred on his horse, which flew down into the enclosed land as if it were mad. To be sure, he himself knew nothing of the uncanny glamour with which the rider of the white horse had been clothed by his former servant boy; but now the people should have seen him, with his eyes staring out of his haggard face, his coat fluttering on his fiery white horse.

Thus summer and autumn had passed and until toward the end of November the work had been continued; then frost and snow had put a stop to the labors and it was decided to leave the land that was to be diked in, open. Eight feet the dike rose above the level of the land. Only where the lock was to be made on the west side toward the water, a gap had been left; the channel up in front of the old dike had not yet been touched. So the flood could make its way into the enclosed land without doing it or the new dike either any great damage. And this work of human hands was entrusted to the great God and put under His protection until the spring sun should make possible its completion.

In the mean time a happy event had been expected in the house of the dikemaster: in the ninth year of his marriage a child had been born. It was red and shrivelled and weighed seven pounds, as new-born children should when they belong, as this one did, to the female sex; only its crying was strangely muffled and did not please the wise woman. The worst of all was that on the third day Elke was seized with high childbed fever, was delirious and recognised neither her husband nor her old helper. The unbounded joy that had come over Hauke at the sight of his child had turned to sorrow. The doctor from the city was called, he sat at her bedside and felt her pulse and looked about helplessly. Hauke shook his head: "He won't help; only God can help!" He had thought out a Christianity of his own, but there was something that kept back his prayer. When the old doctor had driven away, Hauke stood by the window, staring out into the wintry day, and while the patient was screaming in her delirium, he folded his hands—he did not know whether he did so in devotion or so as not to lose himself in his terrible fear.

"The sea! The sea!" wailed the patient. "Hold me!" she screamed; "hold me, Hauke!" Then her voice sank; it sounded, as if she were crying: "Out on the sea, on the wide sea. Oh, God, I'll never see him again!"

Then he turned round and pushed the nurse from the bed; he fell on his knees, clasped his wife and drew her to his heart: "Elke, Elke, don't you know me? I am with you!"

But she only opened wide her eyes glowing with fever and looked about, as if hopelessly lost.

He laid her back on her pillows; then he pressed his hands together convulsively: "Lord, my God," he cried; "don't take her from me! Thou knowest, I cannot live without her!" Then it seemed as if a thought came to him, and he added in a lower voice: "I know well Thou canst not always do as Thou wouldst—not even Thou; Thou art all-wise; Thou must act according to Thy wisdom. Oh Lord, speak to me through a breath!"

It seemed as if there were a sudden calm. He only heard low breathing; when he turned to the bed, he saw his wife lying in a quiet sleep and the nurse looking at him with horrified eyes. He heard the door move.

"Who was that?" he asked.

"Sir, the maid Ann Grethe went out; she had brought in the warming-pan."

"Why do you look at me so in such confusion, Madame Levke?"

"I? I was frightened by your prayer; with that you can't pray death away from anybody!"

Hauke looked at her with his penetrating eyes: "Do you, too, like our Ann Grethe, go to the conventicle at the Dutch tailor Jantje's?"

"Yes, sir; we both have the living faith!"

Hauke made no reply. The practise of holding seceding conventicles, which at that time was in full swing, had also blossomed out among the Frisians. "Down-and-out" artisans and schoolmasters dismissed as drunkards played the leading parts, and girls, young and old women, lazy and lonely people went eagerly to the secret meetings at which anybody could play the priest. Of the dikemaster's household Ann Gerthe and the servant boy in love with her spent their free evenings there. To be sure, Elke had not concealed her doubtful opinion of this from Hauke, but he had said that in matters of faith one ought not to interfere with anyone: this could not hurt anybody, and it was better to have them go there than to the inn for whiskey.

So he had let it be, and so he had kept silent even now. But, to be sure, people were not silent about him; the words of his prayer were spread from house to house. He had denied the omnipotence of God; what was a God without omnipotence? He was a denier of God; that affair with the devil's horse may have something in it after all!

Hauke heard nothing of all this; his ears and eyes were open only for his wife in these days, even his child did not exist for him any more.

The old doctor came again, came every day, sometimes twice, then stayed a whole night, again wrote a prescription and Iven Johns swiftly rode with it to the apothecary. But finally the doctor's face grew more cheerful, and he nodded confidentially to the dikemaster: "She'll pull through. She'll pull through, with God's help!" And one day—whether it was because his skill had conquered her illness or because in answer to Hauke's prayer God had been able after all to find a way out of his trouble—when the doctor was alone with the patient, he spoke to her, while his old eyes smiled: "Lady, now I can safely say to you: to-day the doctor has his gala-day; things looked very darkly for you, but now you belong to us again, to the living!"

Then a flood of light streamed out of her dark eyes; "Hauke, Hauke, where are you?" she cried, and when, in response to her loud cry, he rushed into the room and to her bed, she flung her arms round his neck: "Hauke, my husband—saved! I can stay with you!" then the old doctor pulled his silk handkerchief out of his pocket, wiped his forehead and cheeks with it and nodding left the room.

On the third evening after this day a pious speaker—it was a slippermaker who had once been dismissed by the dikemaster—spoke at the conventicle held at the Dutch tailor's, where he explained to his audience the attributes of God: "But he who denies the omnipotence of God, who says: "I know Thou canst not as Thou wouldst"—we all know the unhappy man; he weighs like a stone on the community—he has fallen off from God and seeks the enemy of God, the friend of sin, as his comforter; for the hand of man has to lean upon some staff. But you—beware of him who prays thus; his prayer is a curse!"

This too was spread from house to house. What is not spread in a small community? And it reached Hauke's ears. He said no word about it, not even to his wife; but sometimes he would embrace her violently and draw her to himself: "Stay faithful, Elke! Stay faithful to me!" Then her eyes would look up at him full of wonder. "Faithful to you? To whom else should I be faithful?" After a short while, however, she had understood his words. "Yes, Hauke, we are faithful to each other; not only because we need each other." Then each went his and her way to work.

So far all would have been well. But in spite of all the lively work, a loneliness had spread round him, and in his heart nestled a stubbornness and a reserved manner toward other people. Only toward his wife he was always the same, and every evening and every morning he knelt at the cradle of his child as if there he could find the place of his eternal salvation. Towards servants and workmen, however, he grew more severe; the clumsy and careless ones whom he used to instruct with quiet reproaches were now startled by his harsh address, and sometimes Elke had to make things right quietly where he had offended.

When spring came, work on the dike began again. The gap in the western dike line was closed by a temporary dike half-moon shaped on the inside and the same toward the outside, for the protection of the new lock about to be made. And as the lock grew, so the chief dike gradually acquired its height, which could be more and more quickly attained. The work of directing was not any easier for the dikemaster, as in place of Jewe Manners, Ole Peters had stepped in as dike overseer. Hauke had not cared to attempt preventing this, but now in place of the encouraging word and the corresponding friendly slap on the shoulder that he had earned form his wife's old godfather, he had to cope with the successor's secret hostility and unnecessary objections which had to be thwarted with equally unnecessary reasons. For Ole belonged to the important people, to be sure, but not to the clever ones in dike matters; besides, the "scribbling hired man" of former days was still in his way.

The brightest sky again spread over sea and marshes, and the enclosed land was once more gay with strong cattle, the bellowing of which from time to time interrupted the widespread calm. Larks sang continually high in the air, but one was not aware of it until for the time of heartbeat the singing had ceased. No bad weather disturbed the work, and the lock was ready with its unpainted structure of beams before it needed the protection of the temporary dike for even one night; the Lord seemed to favor the new work. Then Elke's eyes would laugh to greet her husband when he came home from the dike on his white horse. "You did turn into a good animal!" he said, and then patted the horse's smooth neck. But when he saw the child clinging round her neck, Hauke leaped down and let the tiny thing dance in his arms. Then, when the white horse would fix its brown eyes on the child, he would say: "Come here, you shall have the honor." And he would place little Wienke—for that was her Christian name—on the saddle and lead the white horse round in a circle on the hill. The old ash tree, too, sometimes had the honor; he would set the child on a swinging bough and let it rock. The mother stood in the house door with laughing eyes. But the child did not laugh; her eyes, between which there was a delicate little nose, looked a little dully into the void, and her little hands did not try to seize the small stick that her father was holding for her to take. Hauke did not pay attention to this, especially as he knew nothing about such little children. Only Elke, when she saw the bright-eyed girl on the arm of her charwoman, who had been confined at the same time with her, sometimes said with regret: "Mine isn't as far on as yours yet, Trina." And the woman, as she shook the chubby boy she held by the hand with brusque love, would cry: "Yes, madam, children are different; this one here, he stole apples out of my room before he was more than two years old." And Elke pushed the chubby boy's curls from his eyes, and then secretly pressed her quiet child to her heart.

At the beginning of October, the new lock stood solidly at the west side in the main dike, now closed on both sides. Except for the gaps by the channel, the new dike now sloped all the way round with a gentle profile toward the water and rose above the ordinary high tide by fifteen feet. From the northwestern corner one could look unhindered past Jevers Island out over the sea. But, to be sure, the winds blew more sharply here; one's hair fluttered, and he who wanted a view from this point had to have his cap securely on his head.

Toward the end of November, when storm and rain had set in, there remained only one gap to close, the one hard by the old dike, at the bottom of which the sea water shot through the channel into the new enclosure. At both sides stood the walls of the dike; now the cleft between them had to vanish. Dry summer weather would have made the work easier; but it had to be done anyway, for a rising storm might endanger the whole work. And Hauke staked everything on accomplishing the end. Rain poured down, the wind whistled; but his lean figure on the fiery white horse rose now here, now there out of the black masses of people who were busy by the gap, above and below, on the north side of the dike. Now he was seen below beside the dump-carts that already had to go far on the foreland to get the clay; a crowded lot of these had just reached the channel in order to cast off their loads. Through the splashing of the rain and the roaring of the wind, from time to time sounded the sharp orders of the dikemaster, who wanted to rule here alone to-day. He called the carts according to their numbers and ordered back those that were crowding up. When his "Stop" sounded, then all work ceased. "Straw!" Send down a load of straw! he called to those above, and the straw from one of their loads came tumbling down on to the wet clay. Below men jumped about in it and tore it apart and called up to the others that they did not want to be buried. Again new carts came, and Hauke was up on top once more, and looked down from his white horse into the cleft below and watched them shovel and dump their loads. Then he glanced out over the sea. The wind was sharp and he saw how the edge of the water was climbing higher up the dike and that the waves rose still higher. He saw, too, that the men were drenched and could scarcely breathe during their hard work because of the wind which cut off the air right before their mouths and because of the cold rain that was pouring down on them. "Hold out, men! Hold out!" he shouted down to them. "Only one foot higher; then it'll be enough for this flood." And through all the raging of the storm one could hear the noise of the workmen; the splashing of the masses of clay tumbling down, the rattling of the carts and the rustling of the straw let down from above went on unceasingly. In the midst of these noises, now and then, the wailing of a little yellow dog could be heard, which, shivering and forlorn, was knocked about among all the men and teams. Suddenly a scream of anguish from the little animal rose out of the cleft. Hauke looked down: he had seen the dog hurled down from above. His face suddenly flushed with rage. "Stop! Stop!" he shouted down to the carts; for the wet clay was being heaped up unceasingly.

"Why?" a rough voice bawled up from below, "not on account of the wretched brat of a dog?"

"Stop, I say!" Hauke shouted again; "bring me the dog! I don't want any crime done with our work."

But not a hand stirred; only a few spades full of tough clay were still thrown beside the howling animal. Then he spurred his white horse so that it uttered a cry and stormed down the dike, and all gave way before him. "The dog!" he shouted, "I want the dog!"

A hand slapped his shoulder gently, as if it were the hand of old Jewe Manners, but when Hauke looked round, he saw that it was only a friend of the old man's. "Take care, dikemaster!" he whispered to him. "You have no friends among these people; let this dog business be!"

The wind whistled, the rain splashed, the men had stuck their spades into the ground, some had thrown them away. Hauke bent down to the old man. "Do you want to hold my horse, Harke Jens?" he asked; and the latter scarcely had the reins in his hand when Hauke had leaped into the cleft and held the little wailing animal in his arms. Almost in the same moment he sat high in his saddle again and galloped back to the dike. He glanced swiftly over the men who stood by the teams. "Who was it?" he called. "Who threw down this creature?"

For a moment all was silent, for rage was flashing from the face of the dikemaster, and they had a superstitious fear of him. Then a muscular fellow stepped down from a team and stood before him. "I didn't do it, dikemaster," he said, bit off a piece from his roll of tobacco, and calmly pushed it into his mouth before he went on, "but he who did it, did right; if your dike is to hold, something alive has to be put into it!"

"Something alive? From what catechism have you learned that?"

"From none, sir!" replied the fellow with a pert laugh: "our grandfathers knew that, who, I am sure, were as good Christians as you! A child is still better; if you can't get that, a dog will do!'

"You keep still with your heathen doctrines," Hauke shouted at him, "the hole would be stopped up better if you had been thrown into it!"

"Oho!" sounded from a dozen throats, and the dikemaster saw grim faces and clenched fists round him; he saw that these were no friends. The thought of his dike came over him like a sudden fear. What would happen if now all should throw down their spades? As he glanced down he again saw the friend of old Jewe Manners, who walked in and out among the workmen, talked to this one and that one, smiled at one, slapped another on the shoulder with a pleasant air—and one after another took up his spade again. After a few minutes the work was in full swing—What was it that he still wanted? The channel had to be closed and he hid the dog safely in the folds of his cloak. With a sudden decision, he turned his white horse to the next team: "Let down the straw!" he called despotically, and the teamster obeyed mechanically. Soon it rustled down into the depth, and on all sides all arms were stirring again.

This work lasted an hour longer. It was six o'clock, and deep twilight was descending; the rain had stopped. Then Hauke called the superintendents together beside his horse: "To-morrow morning at four o'clock," he said, "everybody is to be in his place; the moon will still be shining, then we'll finish with God's blessing. And one thing more," he cried, when they were about to go: "do you know this dog?" And he took the trembling creature out of his cloak.

They did not know it. Only one man said: "He has been begging round the village for days; he belongs to nobody."

"Then he is mine!" said the dikemaster. "Don't forget: to-morrow morning at four o'clock!" And he rode away.

When he came home, Ann Grethe stepped out of the door. She had on neat clothing, and the thought shot through his head that she was going to the conventicle tailor's.

"Hold out your apron!" he called to her, and as she did so automatically, he threw the little dog, all covered with clay, into the apron.

"Carry him in to little Wienke; he is to be her companion! But wash and warm him first; then you'll do a good deed, too, that will please God, for the creature is almost frozen!"

And Ann Grethe could not help obeying her master, and therefore did not get to the conventicle that day.

The next day the last cut with the spade was made on the new dike. The wind had gone down; gulls and other sea birds were flying back and forth over land and water in graceful flight. From Jevers Island one could hear like a chorus of a thousand voices the cries of the wild geese that still were making themselves at home on the coast of the North Sea, and out of the white morning mists that spread over the wide marshes, gradually rose a golden autumn day and shed its light on the new work of human hands.

After a few weeks the commissioners of the ruler came with the dikemaster general for inspection. A great banquet, the first since the funeral banquet of old Tede Volkerst, was given in the house of the dikemaster, to which all the dike overseers and the greater landowners were invited. After dinner all the carriages of the guests and of the dikemaster were made ready. The dikemaster general helped Elke into the carriage in front of which the brown horse was stamping his hoofs; then he leaped in after her and took the reins himself, for he wanted to drive the clever wife of his dikemaster himself. Then they rode merrily from the hill down to the road, then up to the new dike, and upon it all round the new enclosed land. In the mean time a light northwest wind had risen and the tide was driven against the north and west sides of the new dike. But one could not help being aware of the fact that the gentle slope made the attack of the water gentler; and praise was poured on the new dikemaster from the lips of the ruler's commissioners, so that the objections which now and then were slowly brought out by the overseers, were soon stifled by it.

This, too, passed by. But the dikemaster received another satisfaction one day as he rode along on the new dike, in quiet, self-conscious meditation. The question naturally arose in his mind, why the new enclosure, which would not have had its being without him, into which he had put the sweat of his brow and his night watches, now finally was named after one of the princesses "the new Caroline-land." But it was so: on all the documents concerned with it stood the name, on some even in red Gothic letters. Then, just as he was looking up, he saw two workmen coming toward him with their tools, the one about twenty paces behind the other. "Why don't you wait!" he heard the one behind calling. The other, who was just standing by a path which led down into the new land, called to him: "Another time, Jens. I'm late; I have to dig clay here."

"Where?"

"Down here, in the Hauke-Haien-land."

He called it aloud, as he trotted down the path, as if he wanted the whole marsh below to hear it. But Hauke felt as if he were hearing his fame proclaimed; he rose from his saddle, spurred on his horse and with steady eyes looked over the wide land that lay to his left. "Hauke-Haien-land! Hauke-Haien-land!" he repeated softly; that sounded as if in all time it could not have another name. Let them defy him as they would—they could not get round his name; the name of the princess—wouldn't that soon moulder in old documents?—His white horse galloped proudly and in his ears he heard a murmur: "Hauke-Haien-land! Hauke-Haien-land!" In his thoughts the new dike almost grew into the eighth wonder of the world; in all Frisia there was not the like of it. And he let the white horse dance, for he felt as if he were standing in the midst of all the Frisians, towering over them the height of a head, and glancing down upon all keenly and full of pity.

Gradually three years had gone by since the building of the dike. The new structure had proved its worth, the cost of repairing had been small. And now almost everywhere in the enclosed land white clover was blooming, and as one walked over the sheltered pastures, the summer wind blew toward one a whole cloud of sweet fragrance. Thus the time had come to turn the shares, which hitherto had only been ideal, into real ones, and to allot to each shareholder the piece which he was to keep as his own. Hauke had not been slow to acquire some new shares before this; Old Peters had kept back out of spite, and owned nothing in the new land. The distribution of the parts could not be accomplished without annoyance and quarreling; but it was done, nevertheless. This day, too, lay behind the dikemaster.

From now on he lived in a lonely way for his duties as farmer and as dikemaster and for those who were nearest to him. His old friends were no longer living, and he was not the man to make new ones. But under his roof was a peace which even the quiet child did not mar. She spoke little, the constant questioning that is so characteristic of bright children was rare with her and usually came in such a way that it was hard to answer; but her dear, simple little face almost always wore an expression of content. She had two play-fellows, and they were enough: when she wandered over the hill, the rescued little yellow dog always jumped round her, and when the dog appeared, little Wienke did not stay away long. The second companion was a pewit gull. As the dog's name was "Pearl" so the gull was called "Claus."

Claus had been installed on the farm by an aged woman. Eighty-year-old Trin Jans had not been able to keep herself any longer in her hut on the outer dike; and Elke had thought that the aged servant of her grandfather might find peaceful evening hours and a good room to die in at her home. So, half by force, she and Hauke had brought her to their farm and settled her in the little northwest room in the new barn that the dikemaster had had built beside the main house when he had enlarged his establishment. A few of the maids had been given rooms next to the old woman's and could help her tonight. Along the walls she kept her old furnishings; a chest made of wood from sugar boxes, above it two coloured pictures of her lost son, then a spinning-wheel, now at rest, and a very neat canopied bed in front of which stood an unwieldy stool covered with the white fur of the defunct Angora cat. But something alive, too, she had had about her and brought with her: that was the gull Claus, which had been attached to her and fed by her for years. To be sure, when winter came, it flew with the other gulls to the south and did not come again until the wormwood was fragrant on the shore.

The barn was a little lower down on the hill, so the old woman could not look over the dike at the sea from her window. "You keep me here as in prison, dikemaster," she muttered one day, as Hauke stepped in to see her, and she pointed with her bent finger at the fens that spread out below. "Where is Jeverssand? Above those red oxen or those black ones?"

"What do you want Jeverssand for?" asked Hauke.

"Jeverssand!" muttered the old woman. "Why, I want to see where my boy that time went to God!"

"If you want to see that," Hauke replied, "you'll have to sit up there under the ash tree. From there you can look over the whole sea."

"Yes," said the old woman; "yes, if I had your young legs, dikemaster."

This was the style of thanks the dikemaster and his wife received for some time, until all at once everything was different. The little child's head of Wienke one morning peeped in through her half-open door. "Well," called the old woman, who sat with her hands folded on her wooden stool; "what have you to tell me?"

But the child silently came nearer and looked at her constantly with its listless eyes.

"Are you the dikemaster's child?" Trin Jans asked, and as the child lowered its head a s if nodding, she went on: "Then sit down here on my stool. Once it was an Angora cat—so big! But your father killed it. If it wee still alive, you could ride on it."

Wienke silently turned her eyes to the white fur; then she knelt down and began to stroke lit with her little hands as children are wont to do with live cats or dogs. "Poor cat!" she said then and went on with her caresses.

"Well," cried the old woman after a while, "now that's enough; and you can sit on him to-day, too. Perhaps your father only killed him for that." Then she lifted up the child by both arms and set it down roughly on the stool. But when it remained sitting there, silent and motionless and only kept looking at her, she began to shake her head. "Thou art punishing him, Lord God! Yes, yes, Thou art punishing him!" she murmured. But pity for the child seemed to come over her; she stroked its scanty hair with her bony hand, and the eyes of the little girl seemed to show that this did her good.

From now on Wienke came every day to the old woman in her room. Soon she sat down on the Angora stool of her own accord, and Trin Jans put small bits of meat and bread which she always saved into the child's little hands, and made her throw them on the floor. Then the gull shot out of some corner with screams and wings spread out and pounced on the morsels. At first the great, rushing bird frightened the child and made her cry out; but soon it all happened like a game learned by heart, and her little head only had to appear in the opening of the door, when the bird rushed up to her and perched on her head and shoulders, until the old woman helped and the feeding could begin. Trin Jans who before never could bear to have anyone merely stretch out a hand after her "Claus," now patiently watched the child gradually win over the bird altogether. It willingly let itself be chased, and she carried it about in her apron. Then, when on the hill the little yellow dog would jump round her and up at the bird in jealousy, she would cry: "Don't, don't, Pearl!" and lift the gull with her little arms so high, that the bird, after setting itself free,

The Rider on the White Horse

would fly screaming over the hill, and now the dog, by jumping and caressing, would try to win its place in her arms.

When by chance Hauke's or Elke's eyes fell upon this strange four-leaved clover which, as it were, was held to the same stem only by the same defect—then they cast tender glances upon the child. But when they turned away, there remained on their faces only the pain that each carried away alone, for the saving word had not yet been spoken between them. One summer morning, when Wienke sat with the old woman and the two animals on the big stones in front of the barn door, both her parents passed by—the dikemaster leading his white horse, with the reins flung over his arm. He wanted to ride on the dike and had got his horse out of the fens himself; on the hill his wife had taken his arm. The sun shone down warmly; it was almost sultry, and now and then a gust of wind blew from the south-southeast. It seemed that her seat was uncomfortable for the child. "Wienke wants to go too!" she cried, shook the gull out of her lap and seized her father's hand.

"Then come!" said he.

But Elke cried: "In this wind? She'll fly away from you!"

"I'll hold her all right; and to-day we have warm air and jolly water; then she can see it dance!"

Then Elke ran into the house and got a shawl and a little cap for her child. "But a storm is brewing," she said; "hurry and get on your way and be back soon."

Hauke laughed: "That shan't get us!" and lifted the child to his saddle. Elke stayed a while on the hill and, shading her eyes with her hand, watched the two trot down the road and toward the dike. Trin Jan sat on the stone and murmured incomprehensible things with her lips.

The child lay motionless in her father's arms. It seemed as if it breathed with difficulty under the pressure of the sultry air. He bent down his head to her: "Well, Wienke?" he asked.

The child looked at him a while: "Father," she said, "you can do that. Can't you do everything?"

"What is it that I can do, Wienke?"

But she was silent; she seemed not to have understood her own question.

It was high tide. When they came to the dike, the reflection of the sun on the wide water flashed into her eyes, a whirlwind made the waves eddy and raised them high up, ever new waves came and beat splashing against the beach. Then, in her fear, her little hands clung round her father's fist which was holding the reins, so that the horse made a bound to the side. The

Theodor Storm

oked up at Hauke in confused fright: "The water, father!
ried.

reed his hand and said: "Be calm, child; you are with your
von't hurt you!"

ɔne pushed her pale blond hair from her forehead and again dared to look upon the sea. "It won't hurt me," she said trembling; "no, tell it not to hurt us; you can do that, and then it won't do anything to us!"

"I can't do that, child," replied Hauke seriously; "but the dike on which we are riding shelters us, and this your father has thought out and has had built."

Her eyes turned upon him as if she did not quite understand that; then she buried her strikingly small head in the wide folds of her father's coat.

"Why are you hiding, Wienke?" he whispered to her; "are you afraid?" And a trembling little voice rose out of the folds of the coat: "Wienke would rather not look; but you can do everything, can't you, father?"

Distant thunder was rolling against the wind. "Hoho!" cried Hauke, "there it comes!" And he turned his horse round to ride back. "Now we want to go home to mother!"

The child drew a deep breath; but not until they had reached the hill and the house did she raise her little head from her father's breast. When Elke had taken off the little shawl and cap in the room, the child remained standing before her mother like a dumb little ninepin.

"Well, Wienke," she said, and shook her gently, "do you like the big water?"

But the child opened her eyes wide. "It talks," she said. "Wienke is afraid!"

"It doesn't talk; it only murmurs and roars!"

The child looked into the void: "Has it got legs?" she asked again; "can it come over the dike?"

"No, Wienke; your father looks out for that, he is the dikemaster."

"Yes," said the child and clapped her little hands together with an idiotic smile. "Father can do everything—everything!" Then suddenly, turning away from her mother, she cried: "Let Wienke go to Trin Jans, she has red apples!"

And Elke opened the door and let the child out. When she had closed it again, she glanced at her husband with the deepest anguish in her eyes from which hitherto he had drawn only comfort and courage that had helped him.

He gave her his hand and pressed hers, as if there were no further need for words between them; then she said in a low voice: "No, Hauke, let me speak: the child that I have borne you after years will stay a child always. Oh, good God! It is feeble-minded! I have to say it once in your hearing."

"I knew it long ago," said Hauke and held tightly his wife's hand which she wanted to draw away.

"So we are left alone after all," she said again.

But Hauke shook his head: "I love her, and she throws her little arms round me and presses close to my breast; for all the treasures of the world I wouldn't miss that!"

The woman stared ahead darkly: "But why?" she asked; "what have I, poor mother, done?"

"Yes, Elke, that I have asked, too, of Him who alone can know; but you know, too, that the Almighty gives men no answer—perhaps because we would not grasp it."

"He had seized his wife's other hand too, and gently drew her toward him. "Don't let yourself be kept from loving your child as you do; be sure it understands that."

Then Elke threw herself on her husband's breast and cried to her heart's content and was on longer alone with her grief. Then suddenly she smiled at him; after pressing his hand passionately, she ran out and got her child from old Trin Jans' room, took it on her lap and caressed and kissed it, until it stammered:

"Mother, my dear mother!"

Thus the people on the dikemaster's farm lived quietly; if the child had not been there, it would have been greatly missed.

Gradually the summer passed by; the migrating birds had flown away, the song of larks was no longer in the air; only in front of the barns, where they pecked at the grain in thrashing time, one could hear some of them scream as they flew away. Already everything was frozen hard. In the kitchen of the main house Trin Jans sat one afternoon on the wooden steps of a stairway that started beside the stove and led to the attic. In the last weeks it seemed as if a new life had entered into her. Now she liked to go into the kitchen occasionally and watch Elke at work; there was no longer any idea of her legs not being able to carry her so far, since one day little Wienke had pulled her up here by her apron. Now the child was kneeling beside her, looking with her quiet eyes into the flames that were blazing up out of the stove-hole; one of her little hands was clinging to the old woman's sleeve, the other was in her own pale blonde hair. Trin Jans was telling a story: "You know," she said, "I was in the service at your great-grandfather's, as housemaid, and there I had to feed the pigs. He was cleverer than all the rest—then it happened—it was awfully long ago—but, one night, by moonlight, they had the lock to the sea closed, and she couldn't go back into the sea. Oh, how she screamed and clutched her hard, bristly hair with her fish-hands! Yes, child,

I saw her and heard her scream. The ditches between the fens were all full of water, and the moon beamed on them so that they shone like silver; and she swam from one ditch into another and raised her arms and clapped what hands she had together, so that one could hear the splash from far, as if she wanted to pray. But, child, those creatures can't pray. I sat in front of the house door on a few beams that had been driven there to build with, and looked far over the fens; and the mermaid was still swimming in the ditches, and when she raised her arms, they were glittering with silver and diamonds. At last I saw her no longer, and the wild geese and gulls that I had not been hearing all the time were again flying through the air with whistling and cackling."

The old woman stopped. The child had caught one word: "Couldn't pray?" she asked. "What are you saying? Who was that?"

"Child," said the old woman; "it was the mermaid; they are monsters and can't be saved."

"Can't be saved!" repeated the child, and a deep sigh made her little breast heave, as if she had understood that.

"Trin Jans!" a deep voice sounded from the kitchen door, and the old woman was a little startled. It was the dikemaster Hauke Haien, who leaned there by the post; "what are you telling the child? Haven't I told you to keep your fairy-tales for yourself or else to tell them to the geese and hens?"

The old woman looked at him with an angry glance and pushed the little girl away. "That's no fairy-tale," she murmured, "my great-uncle told it to me!"

"Your great-uncle, Trin? You just said you had seen it yourself."

"That doesn't matter," said the old woman; "but you don't believe me, Hauke Haien; you want to make my great-uncle a liar!" Then she moved nearer to the stove and stretched her hands out over the flames of the stove-hole.

The dikemaster cast a glance at the window: twilight had scarcely begun. "Come, Wienke!" he said and drew his feeble-minded child toward him; "come with me, I want to show you something outside, from the dike. But we have to walk; the white horse is at the blacksmith's." Then he took her into the room and Elke wrapped thick woolen shawls round the child's neck and shoulders; and soon her father walked with her on the old dike toward the north-west, past Jeverssand, where the flats stretched out broad and almost endless.

Now he would carry her, now she would walk holding his hand; the twilight thickened; in the distance everything vanished in mist and vapour. But in parts still in sight, the invisibly swelling streams that washed the flats had broken the ice and, as Hauke Haien had once seen it in his youth, steaming mists rose out of the cracks as at that time, and there again the uncanny foolish figures were hopping toward one another, bowed and suddenly stretched out into horrible breadths.

The child clung frightened to her father and covered her face with his hand. "The sea devils!" she whispered, trembling, through his fingers; "the sea devils!"

He shook his head: "No, Wienke, they are neither mermaids nor sea devils; there are no such things; who told you about them?"

She looked up to him with a dull glance; but she did not reply. Tenderly he stroked her cheeks: "Look there again!" he said, "they are only poor hungry birds! Look now, how that big one spreads its wings; they are getting the fish that go into those steaming cracks!"

"Fish!" repeated Wienke.

"Yes, child, they are all alive, just as we are; there is nothing else; but God is everywhere!"

Little Wienke had fixed her eyes on the ground and held her breath; she looked frightened as if she were gazing into an abyss. Perhaps it only seemed so; her father looked at her a long while, he bent down and looked at her little face, but on it was written no emotion of her inscrutable soul. He lifted her on his arm and put her icy little hands into one of his thick woollen mittens. "There, my Wienke"—the child could not have been aware of the note of passionate tenderness in his words—"there, warm yourself, near me! You are our child, our only one. You love us—" The man's voice broke; but the little girl pressed her small head tenderly against his rough beard.

And so they went home in peace.

After New Year care had once more entered the house. A fever of the marshes had seized the dikemaster; he too had hovered near the edge of the grave, and when he had revived under Elke's nursing and care, he scarcely seemed the same man. The fatigue of his body also lay upon his spirit, and Elke noticed with some worry that he was always easily satisfied. Nevertheless, toward the end of March, he had a desire to mount his white horse and for the first time to ride along his dike again. This was one afternoon when the sun that had shone before, was shrouded for a long while by dim mist.

In the winter there had been a few floods; but they had not been serious. Only over by the other shore a flock of sheep had been drowned on an island and a piece of the foreland torn away; here on this side and on the new land no damage worth mentioning had been done. But in the last night a stronger storm had raged; now the dikemaster had to go out and inspect everything with his own eyes. He had ridden along on the new dike from the southeastern corner and everything was well preserved. But when he reached the northeastern corner, at the point where the new dike meets the old one, the new one, to be sure, was unharmed. But where formerly the channel had reached the old dike and flowed along it, he saw a great, broad piece of the grassy scar destroyed and washed away and a hollow in the body of the dike worn by the flood, in which, moreover, a network of paths made by mice was exposed. Hauke dismounted and inspected the damage close by: there was no doubt that the mischief done by the mice extended on invisible.

He was startled violently. All this should have been considered when the new dike was being built; as it had been overlooked then, something had to be done now. The cattle were not yet grazing in the fens, the growth of the grass was unusually backward; wherever he looked there was barrenness and void. He mounted his horse again and rode up and down the shore; it was low tide, and he was well aware of how the current had again dug itself a new bed in the clay and had now hit upon the old dike. The new dike, however, when it was hit, had been able to withstand the attack on account of its gentler slope.

A heap of new toil and care rose before the mind's eye of the dikemaster. Not only did the old dike have to be reenforced, its profile, too, had to be made more like that of the new one; above all, the channel, which again had proved dangerous, had to be turned aside by new dams or walls.

Once more he rode on the new dike up to the farthest northwestern corner, then back again, keeping his eyes continually on the newly worn bed of the channel which was marked off clearly on the exposed clay beside him. The white horse pushed forward, snorted and pawed with its front hoofs; but the rider held him back, for he wanted to ride slowly, and to curb the inner unrest that was seething within him more and more wildly.

If a storm flood should come again—a flood like the one in 1655, when property and unnumbered human beings were swallowed up—if it should come again, as it had come several times before! A violent shudder came over the rider—the old dike would not hold out against the sudden attack. What then—what would happen then? There would be only one, one single way of possibly saving the old enclosed land with the property and life in it. Hauke felt his heart stand still, his usually so steady head grew dizzy. He did not utter it, but something spoke within him strongly enough: your land, the Hauke-Haien-land, would have to be sacrificed and the new dike pierced.

In his mind's eye he saw the rushing tide break in and cover grass and clover with its salty, foaming spray. His spur pricked the flanks of his white horse, which, with a sudden scream, flew along the dike and down the road that led to the hill of the dikemaster.

He came home with his head full of inner fright and disorderly plans. He threw himself into his armchair, and when Elke came into the room with their daughter, he rose again, lifted up the child and kissed it. Then he chased away the little yellow dog with a few light slaps. "I have to go up to the inn again," he said, and took his cap from the hook by the door, where he had only just put it.

His wife looked at him anxiously. "What do you want to do there? It is near evening, Hauke."

"Dike matters!" he muttered. "I'll meet some of the overseers there."

She followed him and pressed his hand, for with these words he had already left the door. Hauke Haien, who hitherto had made all decisions by himself, now was eager for a word from those whom he had not considered worthy of taking an interest before. In the room of the tavern he found Ole Peters with two of the overseers and an inhabitant of the district at the card table.

"I suppose you come from out there, dikemaster?" said Ole, who took up the already half distributed cards and threw them down again.

"Yes, Ole," Hauke replied; "I was there; it looks bad."

"Bad? Well, it'll cost a few hundred pieces of sod and a straw covering. I was there too this afternoon.

"It won't be done so cheaply, Ole," replied the dikemaster; "the channel is there again, and even if it doesn't hit the old dike from the north, it hits it from the north-west."

"You should have left it where you found it," said Ole drily.

"That means," returned Hauke, "the new land's none of your business; and therefore it should not exist. That is your own fault. But if we have to make walls to protect the old dike, the green clover behind the new one will bring us a profit above the cost."

"What are you saying, dikemaster?" cried the overseers; "Walls? How many? You like to have the most expensive of everything."

The cards lay untouched upon the table. "I'll tell you, dikemaster," said Ole Peters, and leaned on both elbows, "Your new land that you presented to us is a devouring thing. Everybody is still laboring under the heavy cost of your broad dike; and now that is devouring our old dike too we are expected to renew it. Fortunately it isn't so bad; the dike has held out so far and will continue to hold out. Mount your white horse to-morrow and look at it again!"

Hauke had come here from the peace of his own house; behind these words he had just heard, moderate though they were, there lay—and he could not but be aware of it—tough resistance; he felt, too, as if he were lacking his old strength to cope with it. "I will do as you advise, Ole," he said; "only I fear I shall find it as I have seen it to-day."

A restless night followed this day. Hauke tossed sleepless upon his pillows. "What is the matter?" asked Elke who was kept awake by worry over her husband; "if something depresses you, speak it out; that's the way we've always done."

"It's of no consequence, Elke," he replied, "there is something to repair on the dike at the locks; you know that I always have to work over these things at night." That was all he said; he wanted to keep freedom of action; unconsciously the clear insight and strong intelligence of his wife was a hindrance to him which he instinctively avoided in his present weakness.

The following morning when he came out on to the dike once more the world was different from the one he had seen the day before; it was low tide again, to be sure, but the day had not yet attained its noon, and beams of the bright spring sun fell almost perpendicularly onto the endless flats. The white gulls flew quietly hither and thither, and invisible above them, high under the azure sky, larks sang their eternal melody. Hauke, who did not know how nature can deceive one with her charms, stood on the north-western corner of the dike and looked for the new bed of the channel that had startled him so yesterday, but in the sunlight pouring down from the zenith, he did not even find it at first. Not until he had shaded his eyes from the blinding rays, did he recognise it. Yet the shadows in the twilight of yesterday must have deceived him: it could be discerned but faintly. The exposed mouse business must have done more damage to the dike than the flood. To be sure, things had to be changed; however, this could be done by careful digging and, as Ole Peters had said, the damage could be repaired by fresh sod and some bundles of straw for covering.

"It wasn't so bad," he said to himself, relieved; "you fooled yourself yesterday." He called the overseers, and the work was decided on without contradiction, something that had never happened before.

The dikemaster felt as if a strengthening calm were spreading through his still weakened body and after a few weeks everything was neatly carried out.

The year went on, but the more it advanced and the more undisturbed the newly spread turf grew green through the straw covering, the more restlessly Hauke walked or rode past the spot. He turned his eyes away, he rode on the inside edge of the dike. A few times, when it occurred to him that he would have to pass by the place, he had his horse, though it was already saddled, led

back into the stable. Then again, when he had no business there, he would
wander to it, suddenly and on foot, so as to leave his hill quickly and unseen.
Sometimes he had turned back again, unable once more to inflict on himself
the sight of this uncanny place. Finally, he felt like breaking up the whole
thing with his own hands, for this piece of the dike lay before his eyes like
a bite of conscience that had taken on form outside of himself. And yet his
hand could not touch it any more; and to no one, not even his wife, could he
talk about it. Thus September had come; at night a moderate storm had raged
and at last had blown away to the northwest. On the dull forenoon after it, at
low tide, Hauke rode out on the dike and, as his glance swept over the flats,
something shot through him: there, on from the northwest, he suddenly saw
the ghostly new bed of the channel again, more sharply marked and worn
deeper. No matter how hard he strained his eyes, it would not go.

When he came home, Elke seized his hand. "What's the matter, Hauke?"
she said, as she looked at his gloomy face. "There is no new calamity, is
there? We are so happy now; it seems, you are at peace now with all of
them."

After these words, he did not feel equal to expressing his confused fear.

"No, Elke," he said, "nobody is hostile to me; but it is a responsible
function—to protect the community from our Lord's sea."

He withdrew, so as to escape further questioning by his beloved wife. He
walked through stable and barn, as if he had to look over everything; but he
saw nothing round about. He was preoccupied only with hushing up his
conscience, with convincing himself that it was a morbidly exaggerated fear.

The year that I am telling about, my host, the school-master, said after a
while, was the year 1756, which will surely never be forgotten in this region.
Into the house of Hauke Haien it brought a death. At the end of September
Trin Jans, almost ninety years old, was dying in the barn furnished for her.
According to her wishes, they had propped her up in her pillows, and her
eyes wandered through the little windows with their leaden casements far out
into the distance. A thin layer of atmosphere must have lain above a thicker
one up in the sky, for there was a high mirage and the reflection raised the
sea like a glittering strip of silver above the edge of the dike, so that it shone
dazzlingly into the room. The southern tip of Jeverssand was visible, too.

At the foot of the bed little Wienke was cowering, holding with one hand
that of her father who stood beside her. On the face of the dying woman
death was just imprinting the Hippocratic face, and the child stared
breathlessly on the uncanny incomprehensible change in the plain, but
familiar features.

"What is she doing? What is that, father?" she whispered, full of fear, and dug her finger nails into her father's hand.

"She is dying!" said the dikemaster.

"Dying!" repeated the child, and seemed to have fallen into a confused pondering.

But the old woman moved her lips once more: "Jens! Jens!" her screams broke out, like cries in danger, and her long arms were stretched out against the glittering reflection of the sea; "Help me! Help me! You are in the water——— God have mercy on the others!"

Her arms sank down, a low creaking of the bedstead could be heard; she had ceased to live.

The child drew a deep breath and lifted her pale eyes to her father's. "Is she still dying?" she asked.

"She has done it!" said the dikemaster, and took his child in his arms. "Now she is far from us with God."

"With God!" repeated the child and was silent for a while, as if she had to think about these words. "Is that good—with God?"

"Yes, that is the best." In Hauke's heart, however, the last words of the dying woman resounded heavily. "God have mercy on the others!" a low voice said within him. "What did the old hag mean? Are the dying prophets—?"

Soon after Trin Jans had been buried by the church, there was more and more talk about all kinds of mischief and strange vermin that had frightened the people in North Frisia, and there was no doubt that on mid-Lent Sunday the golden cock was thrown down by a whirlwind. It was true, too, that in midsummer a great cloud of vermin fell down, like snow, from the sky, so that one could scarcely open one's eyes, and afterwards it lay on the fens in a layer as high as a hand, and no one had ever seen anything like it. But at the end of September, after the hired man had driven to the city market with grain and the maid Ann Grethe with butter, they both climbed down, when they came home, with faces pale from fright. "What's the matter? What's the matter with you?" cried the other maids, who had come running out when they heard the wagon roll up.

Ann Grethe in her travelling clothes stepped breathless into the spacious kitchen. "Well, tell us," cried the maids again, "what has happened?"

"Oh, our Lord Jesus protect us!" cried Ann Grethe. "You know, old Marike of the brickworks from over there across the water—we always stand together with our butter by the drugstore at the corner—she told me, and Iven Johns said too—'There's going to be a calamity!' he said; 'a calamity for all North Frisia; believe me, Ann Grethe!' And"—she muffled her voice—"maybe there's something wrong after all about the dikemaster's white horse!"

"Sh! Sh!" replied the other maids.

"Oh, yes, what do I care! But over there, on the other side, it's even worse than ours. Not only flies and vermin, but blood has poured down from the sky like rain. And the Sunday morning after that, when the pastor went to his washbowl, he found five death's heads in it, as big as peas, and everybody came to look at them. In the month of August horrible red-headed caterpillars crawled all over the land and devoured what they found, grain and flour and bread, and no fire could kill them off."

The talker broke off suddenly; none of the maids had noticed that the mistress of the house had stepped into the kitchen. "What are you talking about there?" she said. "Don't let your master hear that!" And as they all wanted to tell about it now, she stopped them. "Never mind; I heard enough; go to your work; that will bring you better blessings." Then she took Ann Grethe with her into the room and settled the accounts of the market business.

Thus the superstitious talk in the house of the dikemaster found no reception from its master and mistress. But it spread into the other houses, and the longer the evenings grew, the more easily it found its way in. Something like sultry air weighed on all, and it was secretly said that a calamity, a serious one, would come over North Frisia.

It was All Saints' Day, in October. During the day a southwest wind had raged; at night a half moon was in the sky, dark brown clouds chased by it, and shadows and dim light flitted over the earth in confusion. The storm was growing. In the room of the dikemaster's house stood the cleared supper table, the hired men were sent to the stables to look after the cattle; the maids had to see if the doors and shutters were closed everywhere in the house and attic, so that the storm would not blow in and do harm. Inside stood Hauke beside his wife at the window, after he had hurriedly eaten his supper. He had been outside on the dike. On foot he had marched out, early in the afternoon. Pointed posts and bags full of clay or earth he had had brought to the place where the dike seemed to betray a weakness. Everywhere he had engaged people to ram in the posts and make a dam of them and the bags, as soon as the flood began to damage the dike; at the northwestern corner, where the old and the new dike met, he had placed the most people, who were allowed to leave their appointed posts only in case of need. These orders he had left when, scarcely a quarter of an hour ago, he had come home wet and dishevelled, and now, as he listened to the gusts of wind that made the windows rattle in their leaden casements, he gazed absently out into the wild night. The clock on the wall was just striking eight. The child that stood beside her mother, started and buried her head in her mother's clothes. "Claus!" she exclaimed crying, "where's my Claus?"

She had a right to ask, for this year, as well as the year before, the gull had not gone on its winter journey. Her father overheard the question; her mother took the child on her arm. "Your Claus is in the barn," she said; "there he is warm."

"Why?" said Wienke, "is that good?"

"Yes, that is good."

The master of the house was still standing by the window.

"This won't do any longer, Elke!" he said; "call one of the maids; the storm will break through the windowpanes—the shutters have to be fastened!"

At the word of the mistress, the maid had rushed out; from the room one could see how her skirts were flying. But when she had loosened the hooks, the storm tore the shutter out of her hand and threw it against the window, so that several panes flew splintered into the room and one of the candles went out, smoking. Hauke had to go out himself to help, and only with trouble did they gradually get the shutters fastened in front of the windows. As they opened the door to step back into the house a gust blew after them so that the glass and silver in the sideboard rattled; and upstairs, over their heads the beams trembled and creaked, as if the storm wanted to tear the roof from the walls. But Hauke did not come back into the room; Elke heard him walk across the threshing floor to the stable. "The white horse! The white horse, John! Quick!" she heard him call. Then he came back into the room with his hair dishevelled, but his gray eyes beaming. "The wind has turned!" he cried, "to the northwest; at half spring tide! Not a wind—we have never lived through a storm like this!"

Elke had turned deadly pale. "And you want to go out once more?"

He seized both her hands and pressed them almost convulsively. "I have to, Elke."

Slowly she raised her dark eyes to his, and for a few seconds they looked at each other; but it seemed an eternity. "Yes, Hauke," said his wife, "I know—you have to!"

Then trotting was heard outside the house door. She fell upon his neck, and for a moment it seemed as if she could not let him go; but that, too, was only for a moment. "This is our fight!" said Hauke, "you are safe here; no flood has ever risen up to this house. And pray to God that He may be with me too!"

Hauke wrapped himself up in his coat, and Elke took a scarf and wrapped it carefully round his neck, but her trembling lips failed her.

Outside the neighing of the white horse sounded like trumpets amid the howling of the storm. Elke had stepped out with her husband; the old ash tree creaked, as if it would fall to pieces. "Mount, sir!" cried the hired man; "the horse is like mad; the reins might tear!"

Hauke embraced his wife. "At sunrise I'll be back."

He had already leaped onto his horse; the animal rose on its hind legs, then, like a warhorse rushing into battle, it tore down the hill with its rider, out into the night and the howling storm. "Father, my father!" a plaintive child voice screamed after him, "my dear father!"

Wienke had run after her father as he was tearing away; but after a hundred steps she stumbled over a mound of earth and fell to the ground.

The man Iven Johns brought the crying child back to her mother. She was leaning against the trunk of the ash tree the branches of which were whipping the air above her, and staring absently out into the night where her husband had vanished. When the roaring of the storm and the distant splashing of the sea stopped for a few moments, she started as if in fright; it seemed to her now as if all were seeking to destroy him and would be hushed suddenly when they had seized him. Her knees were trembling, the wind had unloosed and was sporting with her hair. "Here is the child, lady," John cried to her; "hold her fast!" and pressed the little girl into her mother's arms.

"The child?—I had forgotten you, Wienke!" she cried. "God forgive me!" Then she lifted her to her heart, as close as only love can hold, and with her fell on her knees. "Lord God and Thou my Jesus, let us not be widow and orphan! Protect him, oh, good God; only Thou and I, we alone know him!" Now the storm had no more pauses; it howled and thundered as if the whole world would pass away in this uproar.

"Go into the house, lady!" said John; "come!" and he helped them up and led both into the house and into the room.

The dikemaster Hauke Haien sped on his white horse to the dike. The small path seemed to have no bottom, for measureless rain had fallen; nevertheless, the wet, sucking clay did not appear to hold back the hoofs of the animal, for it acted as if it felt the solid ground of summer beneath it. As in a wild chase the clouds wandered in the sky; below lay the marshes like an indistinct desert filled with restless shadows. A muffled roaring rose from the water behind the dike, more and more horrible, as if it had to drown all other sounds. "Get up, horse!" called Hauke, "we are riding our worst ride."

Then a scream of death sounded under the hoofs of his horse. He jerked back the reins, and turned round: beside him, close above the ground, half flying, half hurled by the wind, a swarm of white gulls was passing by with derisive cackling; they were seeking shelter on land. One of them—the moon was shining through the clouds for a moment—lay trampled by the way: the rider believed that he saw a red ribbon flutter at its throat. "Claus!" he cried; "poor Claus!"

Was it the bird of his child? Had it recognised horse and rider and wanted to find shelter with them? The rider did not know. "Get up!" he cried again; the white horse raised his hoofs to gallop once more. All at once the wind stopped, and in its place there was a deathlike silence—but only for a second, when it began again with renewed rage. But human voices and the forlorn barking of dogs meanwhile fell upon the rider's ear, and when he turned his head round to look at his village, he recognised by the appearing moonlight people working round heaped up wagons on the hills and in front of the houses. Instantly he saw other wagons hurriedly driving up to the higher land; he heard the lowing of cattle that were being driven up there out of their warm stables. "Thank God! They are saving themselves and their cattle!" his heart cried within him; and then with a scream of fear: "My wife! My child! No, no; the water doesn't rise up on our hill!"

A terrible gust came roaring from the sea, and horse and rider were rushing against it up the small path to the dike. When they were on top, Hauke stopped his horse violently. But where was the sea? Where Jeverssand? Where had the other shore gone? He saw only mountains of water before him that rose threateningly against the dark sky, that were trying to tower above one another in the dreadful dusk and beat over one another against the solid land. With white crests they rushed on, howling, as if they uttered the outcry of all terrible beasts of prey in the wilderness. The horse kicked and snorted out into the uproar; a feeling came over the rider that here all human power was at an end; that now death, night, and chaos must break in.

But he stopped to think: this really was the storm flood; only he himself had never seen it like this. His wife, his child, were safe on the high hill, in the solid house. His dike—and something like pride shot through his breast—the Hauke-Haien dike, as the people called it, now should show how dikes ought to be built!

But—what was that? He stopped at the corner between the two dikes; where were the men whom he had placed there to keep watch? He glanced to the north up at the old dike; for he had ordered some there too. But neither here nor there could he see a man. He rode a way further out, but he was still alone; only the blowing of the wind and the roar of the sea all the way from an immeasurable distance beat with deafening force against his ear. He turned his horse back again; he reached the deserted corner and let his eyes wander along the line of the new dike. He discerned clearly that the waves were here rolling on more slowly, less violently; there it seemed almost as if there were a different sea. "That will stand all right!" he murmured, and something like a laugh rose within him.

But his laughter vanished when his eyes wandered farther along the line of his dike: in the northwestern corner—what was that? A dark mass was swarming in confusion; he saw that it was stirring busily and crowding—no doubt, there were people! What were they doing, what were they working for now at his dike? Instantly his spurs dug into the shanks of his horse, and the animal sped thither. The storm rushed on broadside; at times the gusts of wind were so violent, that they would almost have been hurled from the dike into the new land—but horse and rider knew where they were riding. Already Hauke saw that a few dozen men were gathered there in eager work, and now he saw clearly that a groove was dug diagonally across the new dike. Forcibly he stopped his horse: "Stop!" he shouted, "stop! What devil's mischief are you doing there?"

In their fright they had let their spades rest, when they had suddenly spied the dikemaster among them. The wind had carried his words over to them, and he noticed that several were trying to answer him; but he saw only their violent gestures, for they stood to the left of him and their words were blown away by the wind which here at times was throwing the men reeling against each other, so that they gathered close together. Hauke measured the dug-in groove with his quick glance and the might of the water which in spite of the new profile, splashed almost to the top of the dike and sprayed horse and rider. Only ten minutes more of work—he saw that clearly—and the flood would break through the groove and the Hauke-Haien-land would be drowned by the sea!

The dikemaster beckoned one of the workmen to the other side of his horse. "Now, tell me," he shouted, "what are you doing here? What does that mean?"

And the man shouted back: "We are to dig through the new dike, sir, so that the old dike won't break."

"What are you to do?"

"Dig through the new dike."

"And drown the land? What devil has ordered that?"

"No, sir, no devil, the overseer Ole Peters has been here and ordered it."

Rage surged into the rider's eyes. "Do you know me?" he shouted. "Where I am, Ole Peters can't give any orders! Away with you! Go to your posts, where I put you!"

And when they hesitated, he made his horse gallop in among them. "Away to your own or the devil's grandmother!"

"Sir, take care!" cried one of the crowd and hit his spade against the animal that acted as if it were mad; but a kick of its hoof flung the spade from his hand; another man fell to the ground. Then all at once a scream rose from the rest of the crowd—a scream such as only the fear of death can call forth from the throat of man. For a moment all, even the dikemaster and the horse were benumbed. Only one workman had stretched out his arm like a road sign and pointed to the northwestern corner of both dikes where the new one joined the old. Nothing could be heard but the raging of the storm and the roar of the water. Hauke turned round in his saddle: what was that? His eyes grew big: "Lord God! A break! A break in the old dike!"

"Your fault, dikemaster!" shouted a voice out of the crowd; "your fault! Take it with you before the throne of God."

Hauke's face, red with rage, had turned deathly pale; the moon that shone upon it could not make it any paler; his arms hung down limply; he scarcely knew that he was holding his reins. But that, too, was only for a moment. Instantly he pulled himself erect with a heavy moan; then he turned his horse silently, and the white horse snorted and tore away with him eastward upon the dike. The rider glanced sharply to all sides; in his head these thoughts were raging: what fault had he to bear to God's throne? The digging through of the new dike—perhaps they would have accomplished it, if he had not stopped them; but—there was something else that shot seething into his heart, because he knew it all too well—if only, last summer, Ole Peters's malicious words hadn't kept him back—that was the point. He alone had recognised the weakness of the old dike; he ought to have seen the new repairs through in spite of all. "Lord God, yes, I confess it," he cried out aloud suddenly into the storm: "I have fulfilled my task badly."

To his left, close to the horse's the sea was raging; in front of him, now in complete darkness lay the old enclosed land with its hills and homelike houses. The pale light of the sky had gone out altogether; from one point only a glimmer of light broke through the dark. A solace came into the man's heart: the light must have been shining over from his own house. It seemed like a greeting from wife and child. Thank God, they were safe on their high hill! The others surely were up in the village of the higher land, for more lights were glimmering there than he had ever seen before. Yes, even high up in the air, perhaps from the church steeple, light was piercing the darkness. "They must all have left—all!" said Hauke to himself; to be sure, on many a hill the houses will lie in ruins; a bad year will come for the flooded fens; sluices and locks will have to be repaired! We'll have to bear it and I will help even those who did me harm; only, Lord, my God, be merciful to us human beings!"

Then he cast a glance to his side at the new enclosed land; the sea foamed round it, but the land lay as if the peace of night were upon it. An inevitable sense of triumph rose out of the rider's breast. "The Hauke-Haien dike will hold all right, it will hold after a hundred years!"

A thundering roar at his feet waked him out of his dreams; the horse refused to go on. What was that? The horse bounded back, and he felt that a piece of the dike was crashing into the depth right before him. He opened his eyes wide and shook off all his pondering: he was stopping by the old dike; his horse had already planted his forelegs upon it. Instinctively he pulled his horse back. Then the last mantle of clouds uncovered the moon, and the mild light shone on all the horror that was rushing, foaming and hissing into the depth before him, down into the old land.

Hauke stared at it, as if bereft of his senses; this was a deluge to devour beasts and men. Then the light glimmered to his eyes again, the same that he had seen before; it was still burning up on his hill. When he looked down into the land now, encouraged as he was, he perceived that behind the chaotic whirlpool that was pouring down, raging in front of him, only a breadth of about a hundred paces was flooded; beyond he could recognise clearly the path that led through the land. He saw still more: a carriage, no, a two-wheeled cart was driven like mad toward the dike; in it sat a woman—yes, a child too. And now—was that not the barking of a little dog that reached his ears through the storm? Almighty God! It was his wife, his child; already they were coming close, and the foaming mass of water was rushing toward them. A scream, a scream of despair broke forth from the rider's breast: "Elke!" he screamed; "Elke! Back! Back!"

But the storm and sea were not merciful, their raving scattered his words. The wind had caught his cloak and almost torn him down from his horse; and the cart was speeding on without pause towards the rushing flood. Then he saw that his wife was stretching out her arms as if toward him. Had she recognised him? Had her longing, her deathly fear for him driven her out of her safe house? And now—was she crying a last word to him? These questions shot through his brain; they were never answered, for from her to him, and from him to her, their words were all lost. Only a roar as if the world were coming to an end filled their ears and let no other sound enter.

"My child! Oh, Elke, oh, faithful Elke!" Hauke shouted out into the storm. Then another great piece of the dike fell crashing into the depth, and the sea rushed after it, thundering. Once more he saw the head of the horse below, saw the wheels of the cart emerge out of the wild horror and then, caught in an eddy, sink underneath it and drown. The staring eyes of the rider, who was left all alone on the dike, saw nothing more. "The end!" he said, in a low voice to himself. Then he rode up to the abyss where the water, gurgling gruesomely, was beginning to flood his home village. Still he saw the light glimmer from his house; it was soulless now. He drew himself up erect, and drove the spurs into his horse's shanks; the horse reared and would almost have fallen over, but the man's force held it down. "Go on!" he called once more, as he had called so often when he wanted a brisk ride. "Lord God, take me, save the others!"

One more prick of the spurs; a scream from the horse that rose above the storm and the roar of the waves—then from the rushing stream below a muffled sound, a short struggle.

The moon shone from her height, but down on the dike there was no more life, only the wild waters that soon had almost wholly flooded the old land. But the hill of Hauke Haien's farm was still rising above the turmoil, the light was still glimmering there and from the higher land, where the houses were gradually growing darker, the lonely light in the church steeple sent its quivering gleams over the foaming waves.

The story-teller stopped. I took hold of my full glass that had for a long time been standing before me, but I did not raise it to my lips; my hand remained on the table.

"That is the story of Hauke Haien," my host began again, "as I have been able to tell it according to my best knowledge. To be sure, the housekeeper of our dikemaster would have told it differently. For people tell this too: the white horse skeleton was seen after the flood again, just as before, by moonlight on Jevers Island; the whole village is supposed to have seen it. But this is certain: Hauke Haien with wife and child perished in this flood. Not even their graves have I been able to find up in the churchyard; their dead bodies must have been carried by the receding water through the breach into the sea and gradually have been dissolved into their elements on the sea bottom—thus they were left in peace by men at last. But the Hauke-Haien dike is still standing after a hundred years, and to-morrow, if you are going to ride to the city and don't mind half an hour's longer way, your horse will feel it under its hoofs.

"The thanks of a younger generation that Jewe Manners had once promised the builder of the dike he never received, as you have seen. For that is the way, sir: Socrates they gave poison to drink, and our Lord Christ they nailed to the cross. That can't be done so easily nowadays, but—making a saint out of a tyrant or a bad, stubborn priest, or turning a good fellow, just because he towers above us by a head, into a ghost or a monster—that's still done every day."

When the serious little man had said that, he got up and listened into the night. "Some change must have gone on outside," he said, and drew the woolen covering from the window. There was bright moonlight. "Look," he went on, "there the overseers are coming back; but they are scattering, they are going home. There must have been a break in the dike on the other shore; the water has sunk."

I looked out beside him. The windows up here were above the edge of the dike; everything was just as he had said. I took up my glass and drank the rest: "I thank you for this evening. I think now we can sleep in peace."

"We can," replied the little gentleman; "I wish you heartily a good night's sleep."

As I walked downstairs, I met the dikemaster in the hall; he wanted to take home a map that he had left in the tavern. "All over!" he said. "But our schoolmaster, I suppose, has told you a fine story—he belongs to the enlighteners!"

"He seems to be a sensible man."

"Yes, yes, surely; but you can't distrust your own eyes. And over there on the other side—I said it would—the dike is broken."

I shrugged my shoulders. "You will have to think that over in bed. Good night, dikemaster."

The next morning, in the golden sunlight that shone over wide ruin, I rode down to the city on the Hauke-Haien dike.

CPSIA information can be obtained
at www.ICGtesting.com
Printed in the USA
LVHW031100250321
682449LV00003B/137